THE SIEGE OF MORTON'S CROSS

The town leaders of Morton's Cross are awaiting with trepidation the imminent release of Dan McCleery from prison. It is common knowledge that McCleery and his gang of outlaws will want to exact revenge on the townsfolk for incarcerating him five years earlier. But in planning to survive what could become an ugly siege, the town's leaders start falling out with each other. In desperation, they hire bounty hunter Todd McFarlane. For McFarlane to outwit the slippery McCleery, however, the leaders must first step up and face their demons . . .

K. S. STANLEY

THE SIEGE OF MORTON'S CROSS

Complete and Unabridged

LINFORD
Leicester

First published in Great Britain in 2016 by
Robert Hale
an imprint of The Crowood Press
Wiltshire

First Linford Edition
published 2018
by arrangement with
The Crowood Press
Wiltshire

A catalogue record for this book is available
from the British Library.

ISBN 978–1–4448–3825–1

Published by
F. A. Thorpe (Publishing)
Anstey, Leicestershire

Set by Words & Graphics Ltd.
Anstey, Leicestershire
Printed and bound in Great Britain by
T. J. International Ltd., Padstow, Cornwall

This book is printed on acid-free paper

1

Dan McCleery spat the piece of gristle out of his mouth, straight through the bars of his cell window and watched it land on the sill outside.

'Shit!' he exclaimed. He dipped his spoon into his bowl of stew and dragged it around, searching for a decent piece of meat. 'I hate this watered down piss,' he muttered to himself.

For nearly five whole years he had suffered prison food. Five years less three weeks in fact. Those were the three weeks of his stretch he still had left to do. And then, as far as the law was concerned, he had repaid his debt to society — for shooting an unarmed man in the leg and robbing him of his bag of gold.

But as far as Dan was concerned, he had overpaid that debt. The man Dan had shot he swore was up to no good. One of Newt Royston's workers. It was Royston and some of his henchmen who came running at the sound of Dan's gunfire and took down McCleery's horse, breaking Dan's leg in the process. The rest of the McCleery gang returned fire and managed to get away unscathed.

Dan walked over to his cell window. The cell was unbearably hot, as it often was at this time of year, and the light breeze through the iron bars cooled the two beads of sweat rolling down Dan's cheek. Dan looked at the fly sunbathing on the window ledge. He took a mouthful of stew and spat it through the bars at the fly. It was a favourite game of his except, invariably, the fly won and avoided a drowning. But not today. The fly struggled to move its stew coated wings and was temporarily stuck to the window sill. It twitched as a bead of sweat poured off the end of McCleery's nose and landed on its back.

'Got yer, yer bastard!' Dan said to himself. 'An' that's exactly what I'm gonna do to you, Royston, when I get outta here in a few weeks' time. Me an' the boys are gonna piss all over you an' yer two-bit town. Yer gonna wind up dead meat.'

Dan had it all figured out. In fact, he'd had it all figured out, four years and forty-nine weeks ago. In three weeks' time, the boys were gonna meet him on his release from this stinking, rotten jail, and they were gonna ride to Morton's Cross where first he would take his pleasure with his sweet Marie before having a proper meal and a bottle of whiskey. The day after, they'd start shootin' up the town and its officials before hunting down Newt Royston. Then, with Royston and his cronies dead, they could take their time emptying the bank of its cash and valuables. Finally, while Dan helped Marie pack her things and make ready to leave, the boys would torch the town and they'd all ride out together, leaving

Morton's Cross to burn to the ground — not only far richer men than when they arrived but also with the sweet taste of vengeance in their mouths.

* * *

When he was not physically working on his ranch, Newt Royston enjoyed those occasions where he could dress smart and wear one of his stylish suits and leather cowboy boots. It was typical of Newt's extrovert personality; a bold, fearless man, he appreciated life and fully engaged with all aspects of it, which was one of the reasons he was the richest man in Morton's Cross and his opinions were respected by almost all its citizens. The town's mayor, Dwight Farney, frequently sought Newt's private counsel over a glass of whiskey or two on various town matters and this evening was such an occasion.

While Newt looked at the delicate fingers of his beautiful wife as they secured the bootlace tie under the collar of the shirt she had freshly laundered and ironed for him, he realized this particular meeting with Farney could be an awkward one.

The subject was going to be the return of Dan McCleery. Although the citizens of Morton's Cross didn't openly talk about it, everyone was aware of his pending release from prison and privately scared that this hateful man would be seeking his revenge. Not that Newt was one of those. He realized that he was going to be McCleery's main target and was not personally afraid of a fight with McCleery's gang. It would have been fine if the situation had been that simple — a showdown between the two of them — but it was more complicated than that. Potentially a lot more complicated.

First of all, there was the matter of Marie. The last time McCleery was with her she was running the local bordello. So, when he was short of money, which was often, McCleery would act as security at Marie's establishment, for which she gave him a share of the profits. But Newt himself had taken a shine to Marie and married her nearly three years ago. To complete her transition to a respectable woman, she sold the business. So, if on his return to Morton's Cross, McCleery was expecting to have his woman and his old source of income back, he was going to be disappointed.

Secondly, there was the strong possibility that McCleery saw what Newt's employee was actually doing before he tried to run away and ended up being shot and robbed for his trouble. McCleery never raised it at his trial, presumably because either he didn't see it as relevant or thought such an admission would not have helped his case. But five years of doing nothing gives a man plenty of time to pick over the small details of his life and it was clear from the evidence that Dan had been watching his victim at work for quite a while before asking him to hand over the gold. That being the case, he couldn't have failed to notice that Newt's employee was actually taking small nuggets out of his bag and placing them strategically on the ground rather than gathering them up because he had just found them!

It had been a cunning ploy of Newt's to help him find an investment partner for the land he had bought. He had stopped at Morton's Cross a few years ago. His initial intention was to stay for just one night, in the same way that many stagecoach travellers did, either to break their journey west or to switch routes. There was not a lot there then other than the staging post but Newt was somehow drawn to the place and decided to stay on. He took a job as a ranch hand for a while but made his first fortune as a sporting man in the saloons and gambling halls of the farther flung towns. And with this money he purchased some land, on the Dunston Escarpment, about five miles west of the Dry Gulch river valley, and nearly two miles from the western edge of Morton's Cross.

Newt's father had been a farmer and had taught his son a lot about how to find water and irrigate crops in the arid lands of the west, and it was probably that fond boyhood memory that had attracted Newt to put down some roots in the arid district of Morton's Cross. Newt Royston knew that the staging post's geographic location, at a natural crossroads heading north-south and east-west, was the key contribution to giving this small settlement not only an air of permanence but also that its place in history would be secured if it had its own sustainable water supply. So, armed with a few nuggets and handfuls of gold dust that he had won from a miner who was returning east and the knowledge he had learned from his father, he decided to stake a small claim on the Dunston Escarpment.

* * *

His logic was simple; although there were a few trees and plants on his land and one or two small springs, Newt recognized from the general lack of vegetation that Morton's Cross was an area of low rainfall. Yet, five miles to the east, at the bottom of the escarpment, the dry gulch river flowed freely. He reasoned therefore that lying under that five miles of escarpment and probably beyond, there must be an aquifer. People laughed at the idea and as a consequence, Newt was unable to find an investment partner to help shoulder the cost of test drilling a few artesian wells, to prove his theory. People didn't have a vision of how there might be money in water, not least in the same way they had about gold. And that was where Newt's nuggets and dust came in.

He had read in *Roughing It* by Mark Twain about the technique of pocket mining. With this technique, if you are lucky enough to find a very small amount of gold in the dirt at the bottom of an escarpment, you next ask yourself how it came to be there. The likelihood is that it was washed down by the elements, from a richer vein protruding at the edge of the rock face, higher up the escarpment. To find that source you would start at the bottom and move to the left and right of the initial find in a straight line forming the base of a fan shape that would have its handle pointing up the gradient to the richer source. After all, if gold is washed downhill, it spreads out the further down the hill it goes and will naturally settle in a fan shape. The trick therefore is to work out where the perimeters of the fan lie as you work your way across and up the gradient, looking for other small finds. Newt had paid his most loyal men very well to secretly lay the gold, which was what they were doing when the McCleery gang arrived on the scene.

Post McCleery's trial, where incidentally the local jury unanimously found him guilty, Newt continued with his gold pocket mining scheme. With the fan in place, he approached the local mayor, Dwight Farney, and told him he had found a small amount of gold on his land but its positioning suggested there was potentially a large fortune to be had, although that would involve a significant investment in drilling equipment. On visiting the site and seeing the gold for himself, Farney was only too ready to take out his chequebook and pay for exclusive investment rights. Of course, no gold was ever found but after a month, the drills broke through the permeable rock to find the aquifer below, with its filtered water under sufficient pressure to flow back up through the well pipe and pool on the surface.

While McCleery was serving his time in jail, that discovery changed a number of fortunes; first of all, needless to say, there were those of Royston and Farney but more significant was the change in fortune of Morton's Cross itself. The ensuing supply of water enabled local farmland to be developed, which in turn prompted the arrival of the railroad, leading to the expansion of what was once a small settlement into a prosperous town. Last but not least was the change in fortune for Marie, of course. Now, thanks to her husband's unmitigated success, she had become not only a respectable lady but a wealthy one as well.

That left only potentially two flies in the ointment. One was that Newt had effectively conned Dwight. Not that that worried Newt; as far as he was concerned, Dwight was lucky that Newt had chosen him for a 'mark', and as a result made Dwight richer than he could have ever dreamed. But, if he knew what had really happened, the lack of integrity would have seriously concerned Dwight Farney. For Dwight wasn't made like Newt. He was neither a gambler, nor an impulsive decision maker. He certainly wasn't one of those larger than life characters prepared to take on all comers, regardless. Dwight was a man of principle. He had standards for how things should be done and how people should behave. People described his manner as bordering on the evangelistic because Dwight was not shy of 'teaching' people what he regarded as the correct way to behave. The big issue here would be if McCleery had seen the placing of the gold and had worked out during his time in jail, that not only had there been a scam going on but also what it might be. If this was all brought to Dwight's notice, it could drive a large wedge between the two most powerful and influential men in Morton's Cross.

The other potential issue and the biggest human target of any McCleery vendetta was the townsfolk themselves. Angered by their dismissal of him as a 'no good evil chancer' at his trial, it wouldn't be too difficult for the likes of McCleery to work out how to damage the town's water supply, and as a consequence the prosperity upon which the townsfolk of Morton's Cross depended. With these thoughts in his mind, Newt Royston kissed his wife goodbye, mounted the buckboard and made the short journey into town for his meeting with Dwight Farney.

★ ★ ★

Newt was surprised when he walked into Dwight's parlour to find Abe Staunton sitting there. Abe was an old-timer, the only one of the town's original founders still living. When he was a younger man, Abe had been a pony express rider, which was how he discovered the crossroads, and seeing the site's potential, built the settlement's first store. He had long since sold that part of the building but had kept the residential quarters which had been his home for years. Nowadays, Abe spent most of his time sat on his veranda watching the comings and goings at the crossroads. He was regarded as a wise old bird. Not a man to say much but when he did, it was well considered and often insightful. Abe was regarded as one of life's observers and analyzers.

'Ah,' said Dwight, seeing the slight look of surprise on Newt's face. 'I wanted to talk to you about the possible impending arrival of Dan McCleery. I've invited Abe because he has some news about the situation, and besides he always offers wise counsel.'

'Good,' said Newt. 'Well, we might as well start with Abe's news. Go on, Abe, tell us what yer know.'

'Over the last few days, various members of the McCleery gang have been in town. Yer know me, I never forget a face. Mind you, they don't appear to be stayin' over. They arrive an' a little later they leave again. An' sometimes they come back. My guess is they're casin' the joint. Remember, the town's changed a lot over the last five years. I reckon they're making plans, which is why they sometimes come back, presumably to check points of detail.'

'Mm, that doesn't sound good,' Newt responded. 'Me an' my boys will take 'em on, when they finally arrive. We'll deal with 'em, it's probably going to be a bit of a bloodbath, but we'll deal with 'em.'

'That don't sound right to me,' Dwight chipped in quickly. 'We need to be better planned than that. We can't afford a shootout in the middle of town — it's far too crowded, scores of people could get killed.'

'We'll take 'em before they get into town,' Newt said. 'That way no innocent people will get harmed. We'll stage lookouts on each of the four roads. It'll be fine. We don't need to over complicate it.'

'Mm,' said Dwight thoughtfully. 'What d'yer think, Abe?'

'Depends, it's one scenario. But there could be others, we need to think through the possibilities.'

'Good idea,' said Dwight. 'I like that kind of thinking.'

'How d'yer mean, Abe?' Newt asked.

'Well, the out of town fight, assume that they'll all ride in together, as a posse of a dozen men or however big the gang is. They might not choose to do that. They might come in ones and twos over a period of days, for example, and start their attack from inside the town.'

'Good point,' said Dwight, keen to approach the problem in a more scientific way than one, which to his way of thinking was based on sudden impulse.

'If they did that, we would need to pick 'em off in small groups aroun' the town before they could all meet up together,' Newt pointed out. 'We could let Zac Riley have some extra deputies to hunt 'em down an' rough 'em up.'

'I guess a series of small shootouts is better than one big one,' Dwight conceded. 'If any of 'em step out of line for the slightest reason, Riley could sling 'em in jail straight away, which would reduce the amount of shootin'. OK, so that's two possible scenarios; all ride in together an' we deal with 'em before they get into town, or they arrive in town in ones an' twos, so we have small posses to deal with 'em. Are there any other scenarios?'

'Well, we've spoken about us attacking them outside of town but they could by the same token choose to attack us outside of town.'

'How d'yer mean, Abe?' Newt asked, looking slightly puzzled.

'They could attack your water system,' Abe replied. 'Some of your wells use pumps, don't they? They're not all free flow.'

'No, that's right,' said Dwight.

'Well, it's easy,' said Abe. 'Stop the pump, throw poison down the well shaft, followed by dynamite to try and block the shaft an' cut off the water supply. Any water that still flows through will be contaminated. That would all take a lot longer to repair than a damaged overground supply pipe. The supply pipe might appear attractive initially 'cos you would have to try an' secure five miles or so of it, which would take a lot of men, but poison and dynamite would have a bigger impact in the long run.'

'You're right,' said Newt, feeling the anger rise in him. 'We jest don't know what's in that bastard's mind, do we?' he exclaimed, banging his fist down hard on the table.

'Could hire a top gunslinger to try an' infiltrate the gang, so attack 'em from the inside out,' Abe suggested.

'I reckon they'd work that one out pretty quickly if we tried it,' said Dwight.

'Maybe, maybe not,' Abe commented. 'Depends on who it is an' the circumstances surrounding why they might wanna let someone join. Someone with a lot o' confidential information about the vulnerabilities of the town, for example.'

'You thinkin' of Nat Watson, our town planner?' Dwight asked.

'Not specifically Nat,' Abe replied, 'but a top gun fighter who was armed with Nat's knowledge. After all, Nat knows all about the infrastructure of the town, where the water pipes run, the railroad, where the fire risks are, that sort of thing.'

'This is potentially a bigger thing than I imagined,' Newt said.

'Exactly,' said Dwight. 'That's why we must approach it systematically and follow a defined process to recognize all the possibilities, risks and likelihoods and how we might deal with them. The good thing is that we've still got three weeks to do that, so I suggest that we form a defence committee straight away that should consist of the three of us, plus Sheriff Riley and Nat Watson.'

'Agreed,' said Newt, in a resigned tone. 'Agreed.'

2

Dan McCleery lay on his bed smoking a cigarette, the sunlight streaming in through his cell window leaving an enjoyable warm glow on his face. Only two and a half weeks to go now before he would be free and he had already started to increase the number of smokes he had each day. Not only did smoking seem to make the time pass faster but, more importantly, it was an efficient way of destroying the messages his gang had written for him on the inside of the cigarette papers they left on his window sill every other night, securely placed inside the lining of his tobacco pouch.

Dan smiled to himself as he developed his plan of revenge. From the information his gang relayed back as a result of their almost daily reccies of Morton's Cross, he realized how much the town had grown since he was last there. But that worked to his advantage; the larger the place, the easier it would be to hide and create mischief with a far more damaging impact. His basic strategy of rape and pillage remained the same except the new developed town offered more tactical options for delivering the strategy. Ideas were buzzing around in his head.

And then there was his beautiful Marie. All right, she was with another but he would take her back and have her for himself. He wondered if she was still the same — the attentive seductress inside the bedroom; forever helpful and always bending over backwards outside of it to satisfy and win the approval of her man. There were not many women he knew who could and would do that; put her man on a pedestal and look up to him. Dan figured that she may have changed a bit over five years but he knew that her basic personality — an essential part of her allure — wouldn't have changed.

He was starting to realize that he may need to split the gang up and give them separate tasks to do; units operating independently — awareness of what the other units were doing would be on a strict need to know basis. Only Dan would know the master plan and how its separate components pieced together. That way he could co-ordinate operations and assert his leadership authority; it was not uncommon for outlaw gang leaders to find, on release from jail, that their positions had been usurped by a jumped up rival gang member. The only downside of this divide and rule approach to leadership was that he might need to take on one or two new gang members, to fully man the individual units. Obviously there was always a risk in doing this but at the moment the need was not urgent and ultimately depended on how events unfolded.

As always, the timing and place of initial attack would be key and ideally required an element of surprise. He needed more information to finally decide on what this element might be but he had an idea of how he might combine all these factors and gain strategic advantage over the enemy, as he referred to the population of Morton's Cross. He smiled to himself, knowing he would be able to show the world that he was a cunning and formidable opponent. He lay back on his pillow, lit another cigarette and used his imagination to lust after Marie.

*　*　*

Sheriff Zac Riley listened intently to the discussion as his colleagues in the newly formed Morton's Cross Security Association debated how the town should defend itself against the antici-pated revenge attack by the McCleery gang. Some of the ideas he thought outlandish but then again Zac was well known for his cautious approach. He didn't apologize for it because he knew that was what had kept him alive up to

24

now and enabled him to come through some pretty sticky life or death situations involving many an outlaw with a notorious reputation.

It was Nat Watson, the town planner, who was currently in the chair and holding court. Nat's enthusiasm for coming up with new ideas always guaranteed him an audience, even if many of his ideas were impractical. But those that weren't were often real winners and frequently innovative — if not in their design, then in the building and construction process. Watson had a ready-made supporter in Newt Royston. In many respects they were similar; if Royston was the ebullient, down to earth, let's just get on with it type, then Watson was the intellectual version, with his high flying, fancy ideas.

Deep down Zac was suspicious of Newt Royston. Zac had attended every day of Dan McCleery's trial and the fact that a number of Royston's men were on that escarpment with pouches of gold when gold had never been found there previously and certainly not since, didn't quite ring true to him. Zac had never raised it with anyone, because no doubt they would have thought he was being irrational, but it had long since driven how he felt about and reacted to Newt Royston. Zac was suspicious by nature, though; the discovery of a conspiracy never surprised him in the way it did others. What others saw as paranoia he saw as an essential competency for a sheriff who wanted to stay alive. Fortunately for Zac, the Royston-Watson alliance was offset by the more objective, 'scientific' approach of Messrs Farney and Staunton, which meant that Zac didn't need to comment on the wider aspects of the defence plan, just those specific aspects that impacted on him as sheriff.

'So,' said Nat Watson, full of his natural enthusiasm, 'let me try and summarize the key aspects of our plan and let's just check that the various components integrate. The main thrust of the plan is simple and that is to stop the McCleery gang riding into town armed and therefore constructing our main defences outside of the town limits. This gives us just over two weeks to place barbed wire around the well sites and place a permanent armed guard there to prevent sabotage of the town's water supply; and build a security patrol gate across each of the four roads that lead in and out of Morton's Cross. The gates will allow us to stop all traffic approaching town. The gates will be manned by armed patrols, who will be empowered to remove firearms from anyone they don't like the look of and although those individuals will be allowed to enter town, their weapons will be locked in the town armoury and returned to them when they leave. Passengers alighting from the railroad in the middle of town will also be subjected to the same policy. Lastly, we can organize roving patrols that will guard the town limits between the above thoroughfares and also the two-mile water supply pipeline.

'The issues I see are firstly, the roving patrols could use up a lot of manpower and would be stretched, meaning patrols may not be as regular as one would want, and secondly, we do not have much time to test out defences once they are in place. The quicker we build them, however, the more time we have to test them out.'

'Zac. You've been quiet. What do you think in particular about the selective disarmament policy?' Dwight Farney asked his sheriff.

'I'm not sure that selective disarmament would work,' Zac replied. 'The gang could pay cronies to dress respectably and carry arms in. They could come in suited an' booted themselves. We're not gonna recognize all of 'em in that disguise. I think it's all or nothin' — disarm everyone, which I favour, or no one. I know that will make the roving patrols weaker but short of puttin' barbed wire around the whole town, which we don't have time to do, I think we're gonna have to make that compromise.'

'You're right, I think, Zac,' said Abe Staunton. 'If the town was gonna be under siege from an army or a tribe of Indians we would wanna turn it into a fortress if we had the time but we're talkin' about a dozen men here.'

'I take your point, gentlemen,' Dwight Farney said. 'OK then, so we barb wire the wells, build gates and implement a zero tolerance policy for carrying arms within the town limits. Whatever spare resources we have we will use as patrols to rove round the town limits and the supply pipe. All those in favour?' Dwight looked around the room at the raised arms. He banged the gavel down on the table. 'Motion carried.'

★   ★   ★

Dan McCleery lay on his bed, lit another cigarette and flicked the match through his cell window. So, they are building gates and putting barbed wire around the wells to protect themselves. Fools, he thought to himself, smiling at the vulnerabilities of such tactics and how he could exploit them. He knew from a strategic point of view that the leaders of Morton's Cross had failed on the critical success factors for a battle because thanks to his men, McCleery was aware of what defences they were building and where. Little did they know it but the element of surprise, determined by catching the enemy unaware with both the time and place of engagement, was gone for them. McCleery sent word for units one and two of his gang to be ready to move a week earlier than his release from jail.

3

McCleery's men dismounted on the edge of the woods, protected by the tree line. They said nothing, each man silently thinking about the task that lay ahead. The ride out to the pipeline had been uneventful, as they had expected since the journey involved carving out a virgin route through the woodland. The leader of the small band pulled a map from his pocket and laid it on the ground. He took a telescope from his saddle-bag and looked out to the west. Dusk was starting to turn into night, making it difficult to see much, but he could make out the rising line of the Dunston Escarpment. He estimated that the wells were less than a mile away. No doubt there would be gangs of men up there, even at this late hour, fencing in the area and guarding the well heads. The pipeline would be about a quarter of a mile straight ahead, lying exposed on the surface of open but unmanned country.

He turned rapidly as one of his men tapped him on the shoulder and pointed out the lights about half a mile away to the east. There were two of them about a hundred yards apart, moving slowly up the escarpment, heading in their direction away from Morton's Cross. He surmised that they were lanterns. They appeared to sway slightly, across the axis of their forward direction, suggesting that they were being carried by riders on horseback. The leader grunted.

This torch party represented an unexpected obstacle for him. He only had three other men in his team but the torch party was still too far away for him to determine how many members made up its number. He wondered what its purpose might be. If they were bringing supplies from the town to the well head, he would have thought they would have just followed the pipeline and not needed to make their presence so conspicuous. On the other hand, they may have been an inspection team checking the pipe for signs of wear or damage. Nothing suspicious about that, he reasoned. After all, if the pipe started leaking, eventually the water pressure would reduce and people would notice, demanding restoration of the supply.

The leader convinced himself that whatever the torch party was doing out there in the open it was just some routine activity. He and his men should be able to deal with them if necessary, they wouldn't be up against hired guns. One option was to let them ride past unencumbered and wait until they were long gone. The trouble with that plan would be that he and his gang would have to be patient and wait a long time before they could get on with their task. The alternative would be to take the torch party on but the leader could only afford to lose two men at the very most and in reality the loss of any of his gang could put successful execution of their task at risk. He decided to wait until he could get a better view on the make-up of the torch party before committing to action. In fifteen minutes' time he would be able to make a far more accurate assessment of what they might be up against. He signalled to his men to lie low and put out their cigarettes until further notice.

★   ★   ★

'Thought I saw a light over there, Bram,' one of the torch party called out.

'What kinda light?' Bram asked.

'Dunno. Bit like a match flaring up as if someone was lightin' a cigarette.'

'Odd,' Bram commented. 'Where-abouts?'

'Over there. On the edge of the woods.'

'Surprised, if there is anyone out there. Bit of a wilderness,' Bram responded.

'Yer don't think it's McCleery's gang,

do yer, boss?' said the third member of the torch party.

'Naw, doubt it,' Bram replied. 'McCleery ain't due out of jail for a few days yet. Still, guess we'd better go an' take a look. Let's put these lanterns out an' not make ourselves look too obvious.'

Bram led his two colleagues away from the pipeline and towards the edge of the woods. They rode at a walking pace. As they got closer to the edge of the woods, Bram could make out the light of a cigarette. As he entered the wood, he could see in the distance four horses tethered to the trunk of a tree. He should have thought the situation a little odd; four horses, a solitary cigarette smoker and no camp fire. But he didn't. He and his men took two bullets each.

The post mortem showed that three of the bullets were fired down into their chests and at an angle, the most likely explanation being they were attacked by gunmen hiding up above in the trees, while the other three bullets hit entered their stomachs at 180 degrees, suggesting their adversaries were standing on the ground when they pulled their triggers, presumably hiding in the bushes. Whatever way the coroner looked at it, he ended up concluding that Bram and his torch party had been caught in a very well organized ambush.

★ ★ ★

The leader and his men left the fallen bodies of the torch party on the ground, mounted their horses and rode out to the pipeline. They wrapped a belt of explosive around one of the joints before covering the pipe either side of the joint with mounds of earth. Not only would this quell the impact of the explosion as much as possible but also maximize their getaway time. They ran the fuse wire to the edge of the woods and were on their way north before the flame had reached the explosive. By the time they had reached their destination, a small settlement ten miles to the north-west of Morton's Cross, the people of Morton's Cross were complaining that the pressure of the water supply was dwindling fast. It wasn't until much later on, when the leader and his men were asleep in bed after a late night of partying and gambling that Newt Royston's boys found the damaged pipeline underneath an expansive deep pool of muddy water.

★   ★   ★

Chaos had ensued in Morton's Cross once the people of the town discovered they had no water. The first places to realize were the hotels, whose proprietors were greeted by angry kitchen staff unable to wash up or boil food, and angry patrons unable to take a bath. The increasing bedlam spread to the whore houses, the saloons and gambling halls and eventually the railroad. Unable to supply water for the railroad's locomotives, the trains stopped running, with passengers neither able to enter the town or leave. More important, the seemingly never ending supplies of food, drink, clothes, household items, machinery and equipment, the very life blood of Morton's Cross that flowed into its heart through the veins of the railroad network, would soon dry up once existing stocks had been exhausted or worn out. This impending situation was a call to arms for two opposing groups of people.

Newt Royston had already sprung into action. He didn't wait for his partner, Dwight Farney, to call an extraordinary meeting of the Morton's Cross Security Association. The time for discussing principled action had passed. He had ridden out to his ranch and rounded up as many of his men as possible. He then divided them into two teams; the first team was to ride at full speed out to the well head and turn off the flow and then track back towards Morton's Cross along the pipeline, looking for any sign of rupture. The second team was to check the pipeline from the Morton's Cross end.

Newt Royston left the townsfolk in no doubt as to his plans to sort out the damage. Unfortunately, their number included some of the opposing group — McCleery's men. They stopped whatever pleasure they were engaged in at the time, individually collected their weapons from the town armoury and met up on the western road to Royston's ranch. By the time they arrived at the large ranch house, Royston and his men were long gone into the black of the night. They skirted cautiously around the ranch to see who might be left. There were still lights on in various rooms, not only in the main house but in the various outbuildings. This indicated either the continuing presence of a large number of the normal occupants or, more likely, that most of them had left and had been in much of a hurry to do so.

★ ★ ★

Marie Royston was blissfully unaware of what might be going on outside. She knew her husband had left in a rush and taken many of the ranch workers with him.

'Problem with the town water supply,' he had said on the way out. 'Needs fixin', right away.'

Problems of a technical or systems nature were not Marie's forte, the only problems she could relate to were people ones. So, she had bid him farewell and he left her in the righteous company of the town preacher. The preacher man had only recently arrived in Morton's Cross and was doing the rounds of the local great and the good in order to gain a better understanding of his new flock and their levels of spiritual awareness.

Marie felt a little overawed that a 'servant of God' was deferring to her opinion on such spiritual matters. She of all people, a one time good time girl, whose standing in the local community had changed virtually overnight thanks to her marriage to Newt Royston, the baron of the area. But she needn't have felt nervous as her personality would see her through — it always had, ever since she was a small girl. She had learnt from an early age that the way to get people to warm to her was to make them feel good about themselves by her ability to respond to their feelings. Although occasionally she wondered if she had buried her own true feelings in her desire to please others, she accepted that the human condition was one of compromise and that perfection was elusive. Measured against those standards, her approach to relationships was a successful one, bringing her material security and, since her marriage, emotional security as well. In fact, her husband often remarked on how he saw her as the 'good woman' behind his 'great man', the power behind his throne. Not that she could claim to always have been an angel and deny that some of the more salubrious aspects of her past were not of her own making. On the one hand her generous, open hearted and enthusiastic nature had made her very popular but on the other, it had given her the opportunity to learn how to manipulate and seduce people to get what she believed she wanted. Dan McCleery had been a case in point.

The preacher, however, was remarkably impressed by this woman and Marie was flattered to hear him say so.

'I have nothing but the highest regard for you, madam,' he told her. 'After all, it is very few who see the light on the road to Damascus and are able to turn themselves around as a result. Only they are then able to focus on using the good side of their characters to spread light and love and stop being a slave to their darker side,' he said with the authority of someone who understood the sort of content that makes a good sermon.

'Why thank you, Preacher, thank

you,' said Marie. 'You are clearly a good man. I feel at ease with you.'

Indeed, he felt he had a natural rapport with Marie; they were both empathetic characters, willing to adjust their own behaviours to fit in with others, albeit that he recognized, or more accurately partially recognized, that his own faults, for example at times being wilful (which he justified as enacting God's will) and on occasion being indecisive, as he was about to demonstrate, were perhaps different.

A sudden commotion outside caused Marie and the preacher to break off from their indulgence in mutual flattery.

'What is going on?' the preacher asked, failing to mask the note of concern in his voice. Marie walked to the window and poked her head through a gap in the curtains.

'My god!' she exclaimed. 'The barn and some of the out-houses are on fire!'

'Are we safer in here or outside?' the preacher asked.

'I don't know. The few workers that Newt didn't take with him are trying to put out the fires,' Marie replied. 'I think we should go outside and stand well away from the buildings.'

'Goin' somewhere?' A man with a gruff voice and a neckerchief pulled up over his mouth and nose stood in the doorway, blocking their exit. He was brandishing a flaming torch. Instinctively but uncharacteristically, the preacher pulled out a pistol from under his frock coat. 'Drop that, Preacher,' said the man with the gruff voice, 'or the whole house'll go up in smoke if yer pull that trigger and I fall.'

Characteristically, the preacher froze. Would that happen if he pulled the trigger? Shouldn't he try and negotiate first rather than shoot a man in cold blood? Wouldn't that be God's way? He let his weapon fall to the ground. A second man entered the room, gun already drawn. He smashed its butt against the preacher's head. The preacher fell to the ground like a sack of potatoes.

'Well, hello, Marie,' the gunman said.

She recognized him immediately. She had slept with him for money a number of times in her former life. He was one of McCleery's men. In fact, it was through this particular low life that she had met Dan McCleery.

The man grabbed hold of her and pulled her towards the door. 'Did you get the stuff from the safe?' he asked his colleague with the gruff voice.

'Yes,' the man replied. 'Shall I torch the house?'

'No,' replied the gunman. 'To do that and murder the preacher in the process would not be in our long term interests. Anyway, we got everythin' we came for.'

4

Dan McCleery whistled merrily to himself as the stage pulled into Maryville, a small, one street town, forty miles north-west of Morton's Cross. For the last thirty miles he had travelled by himself, the other passengers having disembarked at various places en route. Under normal circumstances he would have dozed off, but today, the day of his release from a five-year jail term, he was wide awake. Five years in a small cell meant that his sleep account was in credit and he was able to savour that strange feeling of unity with nature once again — the joy of freedom.

The stagecoach pulled up outside the Maryville hotel. The hotel porter ran down the boardwalk steps and signalled to the driver and his shotgun rider to load a small trunk on to the coach roof.

A woman appeared at the top of the steps and watched the loading of the trunk with a critical eye — it was clearly her luggage. Satisfied that it had been handled with due care, she opened the door of the stage, hoisted up her black skirts and climbed in. She brushed the dust off the seat opposite McCleery, turned round and sat down. An unusually attractive looking woman, she had an air of mystery about her and McCleery couldn't fathom whether it was her dark hair that flowed in ringlets on to her shoulders, her large green eyes or the bright colours in her shawl that stood out against her dark dress. She exuded an air of confidence that made her difficult to age; her skin suggested she was probably thirty or thereabouts but her mannerisms implied the maturity of someone older. She smiled briefly at McCleery before taking a book out of her bag and starting to read.

McCleery noticed the cover of the

book. 'Shakespeare,' he said. 'You read Shakespeare?'

The woman looked up and put her book, face down on her lap.

' 'But, soft! what light through
        yonder window breaks?
It is the east, and Juliet is the sun.
Arise, fair sun, and kill the envi-
        ous moon,
Who is already sick and pale with
        grief,
That thou her maid art far more
        fair than she'.'

'Very good,' said McCleery. 'Very good indeed. I am impressed. *Romeo and Juliet.*'

'You know it,' said the woman. 'Well, I am impressed also.'

'My mother was an actress once,' McCleery said. 'An' I have done time in jail, so I have had plenty of time to familiarize myself with the great William Shakespeare. Does that worry you?'

'What?' the woman asked.

48

'That I have done time in jail.'

'Only if you think it should,' the woman replied, somewhat indifferent to McCleery's foibles and failings. 'An educated outlaw, eh? I find that intriguing, not worrying. The real man lies in his breeding, not his misde-meanours.'

'Thank you, ma'am. Dan McCleery at your service. And you are?'

'Trixie-Lou Sanders,' the woman replied. 'Not one time actress, but all the time actress.'

She laughed at her joke although she knew it to be true. If McCleery was testing her level of vulnerability, she knew her self-confidence would have disappointed him. Besides, she always carried a small gun in her garter and could easily slip into the role of femme fatale, as she had on numerous occasions. The suspicious moment passed.

'An' where might you next be performin', ma'am?' McCleery asked.

'In the theatre at Morton's Cross. A

variety show; bit of Shakespeare, bit of poetry, singing and dancing, you know the sort of thing. Twice nightly, except Sunday for the next week,' Trixie-Lou explained. 'You should avail yourself of tickets,' she added.

'I jest might do that,' Dan replied. 'I plan to spend some time in Morton's Cross over the next few days.'

'I trust it's not outlaw business,' Trixie-Lou commented. 'Not good for the soul, you know. The lighter your heart, the more you will enjoy the show.'

'No, it's not. I have a few affairs to put in order first and then I'm gonna be lookin' for a new business partner,' Dan said. 'See meself these days as more of an entrepreneur.'

'And what line of entrepreneurial business might that be, Mr McCleery? Would it interest a working girl like me?'

McCleery didn't know whether the last sentence was intended as some sort of innuendo or not. One thing for sure was that this woman knew how to get under a man's skin and start weeding things out of him that might be better left undisturbed. He decided to close down the conversation without giving too much away but keeping it authentic.

'Oh, I'm contemplatin' working with the earth's natural resources,' he said. 'You know, mining, the land, that sort of thing.'

'Forestry, farming, fishing, mining,' Trixie-Lou said. 'I know the sort of thing — you an' everybody else. I wish you luck.' She turned her attention back to her book and then closed her eyes as if she was entering some sort of trance state of contemplative meditation. She clearly had no interest in the bland nor the routine, McCleery thought to himself; an interesting woman.

Her return to full consciousness, half an hour or so later, caught McCleery unawares.

'We've stopped. Are we nearly there yet?' she asked.

51

He quickly regained his composure as if his attention had never wandered and he had been sat there in silence, only waiting to respond to her next few words.

'I think we are in a queue,' he answered, 'waiting to hand in our firearms before we are allowed through the town gates.'

'Firearms, town gates?' she enquired. 'I didn't know this was Dodge City. I thought Morton's Cross had a good reputation.'

'It does,' Dan reassured her. 'It's, how d'yer say, preventative. They have a good reputation and they don't wanna lose it. The gates are an insurance policy.'

'You seem well informed, Mr McCleery,' Trixie-Lou said.

'Make it my business to know what is goin' on, ma'am,' McCleery replied. The coach ground to a halt and a man wearing a revolver and carrying a rifle opened the door of the stagecoach.

'Morton's Cross is a peaceful town.

Any weapons to declare and hand over?' he asked brusquely. 'Knives, pistols, that kind of thing. You can pick 'em up from the armoury when you leave town. Your trunk on the roof, ma'am? We'll need to get that down and check what's inside.'

'Be my guest,' Trixie-Lou said with indignation.

'Sir?'

'Two six-guns, here in me bag and a belt of ammunition,' McCleery said as he handed them over.

The man took them and looked McCleery straight in the eyes, thinking that he knew the face. 'Wait here,' he said and scurried off. The coach driver and his shotgun rider unloaded Miss Sanders's trunk and placed it at the side of the road. The man who had taken McCleery's guns returned with a colleague, distinguished by the tin star on his chest.

'Why, if it ain't Zac Riley,' exclaimed McCleery, 'sheriff of these parts.'

'We've been expectin' you, McCleery,'

Zac said in an authoritative tone. 'I warn yer that yer not particularly welcome in these parts. How long yer stayin' for?'

'Coupla days maybe. You can't run me out of town, Riley. I'm a free man. I ain't done nothin' wrong,' McCleery pointed out calmly.

'An' make sure yer don't,' Zac retorted. 'If yer wan' my advice, I suggest that yer stay out of trouble an' keep a low profile aroun' here. We'll attend to yer trunk shortly, ma'am,' he said, talking to Trixie-Lou while shutting the stagecoach door. She slumped back in her seat and crossed her legs. Her skirt fell open, revealing her left thigh. McCleery noticed the small pistol protruding from her garter. Seeing a knowing look on his face, she threw the loose material of her skirt over her leg to cover herself.

'You showgirls like to pack a pistol, don't yer?' McCleery said, smiling. 'Yer supposed to hand that in, yer know.'

'Many girls see carryin' a pistol on their person as a woman's privilege. In my profession, I see it as a woman's right. Anyway it's only a stage prop. Ain't gonna do no one any harm,' she said, attempting to reduce the seriousness of her dishonesty.

'Mm,' Dan McCleery murmured. 'You might have a gun up your skirts but I fancy you have even bigger secrets up your sleeve.'

'My secrets are just those of tainted love, Mr McCleery. I suspect yours are of a far more villainous nature than mine.'

'Maybe we should stay close,' Dan suggested. 'Watch each other's backs.'

'Maybe,' she heard herself saying.

★   ★   ★

Marie Royston looked out from her prison window. She was being held in a cave, somewhere out in the middle of the Badlands, west of Morton's Cross. It was arid country with little vegetation, very few natural sources of food and even fewer of water. There was no resident population. The only people who might stay overnight were itinerants who were either temporarily using the Badlands as a place to hide or those taking a shortcut between the scene of their last crime and the site of their next one. Her captors had rolled a large water barrel out to their camp and they took it in turns to ride ten miles to the nearest spring to keep it topped up. Other than that, they had stockpiled sufficient quantities of food, tobacco and whiskey to stay hunkered down in the area for the best part of a month.

The men slept in the open but had gone to some trouble to minimize Marie's discomfort. They had supplied blankets for bedding as the nights could be very cold and would often light a small fire for her on a ledge at the back of the cave. The smoke would be drawn up the back wall and exit the cave roof through gaps in the rock, which also acted as a source of light from the outside world. The gaps were small, however, and certainly not wide enough for someone to enter or exit the cave. And then there was the door of her rock cell. Someone had gone to a lot of trouble to build a solid wood frame and hang the made to measure door complete with an iron grille window.

They had also put a lot of thought into this particular door's main purpose, that of providing security. The door had four bolts; two on the outside and two on the inside. The reason for the ones on the outside were obvious to Marie, as were the ones on the inside, once one of her captors had told her that they had been put there so that she could protect herself from any unwanted advances of her captors. The thinking had all the hallmarks of Dan McCleery. He was always one step ahead of everybody else. Marie took partial reassurance from it. At least it meant that Dan placed value on her well-being, that she was worth something. The question was, did he place more value on her for his own personal needs or was it because he realized what her value might be worth to somebody else? Or was it both? Sometimes the thought depressed her and at other times it gave her hope. At least for the time being she could take succour from the fact that she knew her formidable husband, Newt Royston, would be moving heaven and earth to try to find her.

* * *

'What do you mean you allowed that bastard McCleery to walk back into this town! Are you mad?' Royston stared daggers at Sheriff Zac Riley. The other members of the Security Association sat in silence, stunned by Newt's out-burst.

'I had no option,' Riley spat back straight away. 'The man has not been charged with breaking any law. Any court in the land would throw out a charge of kidnapping your wife and burning down half your spread through lack of hard evidence based on a watertight alibi that McCleery was in jail at the time! The fact that we all suspect that he was behind those . . . those heinous crimes, is not even circumstantial at this stage — it's pure bloody conjecture 'cos we can't damn well prove a thing!' The room erupted in a maelstrom of unbridled emotion.

'Gentlemen, gentlemen!' shouted Dwight Farney. 'Order, order, please. Having a slanging match ain't gonna get us any closer to sorting out this problem!'

The noise subsided as emotions were brought under control. There was enough brain power assembled in the room to realize that emotions needed to be put on hold. Only clear thinking was going to resolve this problem, if it could be resolved. The clearest thinker in the room signalled to the chair that he wanted to speak.

'Go on, Abe,' responded Dwight Farney. 'What d'yer wanna tell us?'

'We might be able to find Marie by ourselves, we might not but we would stand a better chance with outside help.'

'How d'yer mean, Abe?' Newt asked.

'The problem with us is that we're too emotionally involved. Also, we have other distractions that we need to attend to, yer know, our land, the town and so on. We don't have the time or energy to devote the amount of effort to this task that it probably requires. An' that's nobody's fault. Findin' people is not what any of us do fer a livin' an' if yer don't mind me sayin' so, Zac, it ain't what you do, either, well, not full-time anyway.'

'An' who does, Abe? D'yer know of anyone?' Dwight asked.

'Yes, I do,' replied Abe. 'There's a man I used to know a few years back. Lives up north but I heard he's still in the game an' he's good. In fact, he's very good.'

'What game might that be?' Newt asked in a despairing tone.

'Bounty huntin',' Abe replied. 'He's good at findin' people 'cos that's all he does. In particular, he's good at findin' bad people. His name's Todd McFarlane. D'yer wan' me to make contact?' The room was abuzz with the sound of expectation.

5

Todd McFarlane sat at the back of the saloon in the foyer of the Eagle Theatre. This was an unusual job in that his supposed prey, Dan McCleery, was sat less than thirty yards away from him. But McCleery was only a suspect and, according to Sheriff Riley, had been in town for nearly a week now and hadn't put a foot wrong. It was possible, as Riley had pointed out in his briefing, that McCleery might not be the one behind the damaging of the town's water supply and the kidnapping of Marie Royston. Even the use of the word kidnap was conjecture. Marie could be dead, after all there had been no news of her nor any sign of a ransom note.

McFarlane knew different, however. Not because he had any solid evidence but because his gut told him so and experience had taught him to trust his gut every time. Everything about McCleery smacked of a bad man, from the way he looked, the way he looked at others, his whole body language said that he was just another drifter looking for someone to exploit. McFarlane knew. He had made a good living from tracking down men of this type. And from the way McCleery was looking into the woman's eyes with whom he was sharing a pre-show drink, McFarlane knew this guy was a sleaze ball as well.

Any expert people watcher, which McFarlane was, would have seen that the leading lady of this review had got Dan McCleery well and truly on the end of her hook. It was plain to see that while McCleery was smitten, Trixie-Lou Sanders was toying with him, playing a game. The wrong word or move on McCleery's part and Sanders would drop him like a stone, but the right word or move and she might allow him to enjoy her as a prize. And then,

McFarlane realized, the show would close and the mysterious, sultry Miss Trixie-Lou would leave town, and probably any relationship she might have with McCleery would be over also. He was just a short-term muse for a woman like her — an amusement, a distraction on the road, until the next show, the next town. So McCleery would also leave Morton's Cross but, unlike her, he would be angry. Especially if Miss Sanders's attention had caused him to delay his little kidnapping business on the pretext of an assignation that later was not fulfilled. But that anger could cause him to make mistakes in covering his tracks. A satisfied man would be focused on the task in hand.

Todd McFarlane realized that he would need to break the two of them up sooner rather than later to make sure McCleery's lascivious nature was not fulfilled on this occasion. The bell rang, signalling the final show was about to start, so McFarlane went into the theatre and stood at the back with Zac Riley while McCleery took his seat in the middle of the front row.

★ ★ ★

Although Marie Royston wasn't going to take the risk, she probably could sleep safely in her cave cell without bolting the door. She had expected sight of Dan McCleery a few days ago and his prolonged absence was not only making her angry but she was starting to think that he wasn't involved in this caper and it was run and organized by a splinter group from his old gang. Her original plan if Dan had turned up a few days ago would have been to manipulate and tempt him, possibly seduce him if necessary, to secure her release. But that strategy was no longer viable and it was the realization of that which was at the root of her anger.

Her captors would take it in turns to ride off somewhere and refresh themselves but she was afforded no such luxury. Water was on ration at the site of her imprisonment and only used for drinking in order to stay alive. As a result, her clothes were dirty, her hair greasy and matted and she had begun to smell. At least no man was going to try it on with her. Under stress, her personality had become the opposite of who she normally was. She demanded that she supervise the cooking of her food, and when her guard, who was slightly scared by this 'mad woman' as he thought she had become, obliged, she spat the food out in his face.

That night her mood changed dramatically again. Secure in her cell, she lay down and sobbed her eyes out until her tear sacks had run dry and her heaving body became exhausted. Death seemed preferable to this living hell yet she didn't feel suicidal. But if death was imminent, an inescapable result of her situation, then she was going to face it, prepare for and own the process.

It turned into a metamorphosis for Marie. She had always made her journey through life by responding to others' needs, being in service, her reward being their gratitude. As a result, she had denied her own true identity and the slow, painful under-standing of that fact, the feeling of emptiness at a life denied, enabled her to feel her true nature and at peace with the world. When she awoke the next morning she felt re-energized and ready to act on her own feelings and desires.

★ ★ ★

'Unhand me, sir! Take my money, if that's what you want!' The crowd cheered as Trixie-Lou played up to the audience, striding purposely across the stage, her arms outstretched towards them, her head flung back in a classic dramatic pose. Her male lead tore her bag from her hand. The crowd cheered again as Trixie-Lou pulled back her dress to show a long leg. Her garter revealed, she removed a small pistol from the holster strapped around her thigh and turning towards her fellow thespian, pulled the trigger. There was a blinding flash, a loud bang and, as the smoke cleared, the actor's hat lay on the stage, having been blown clean off his head. The crowd cheered again.

'The lady can shoot,' Zac Riley commented.

'Sure can,' Todd replied. 'Left hander as well. Is that gun on your manifest? The only guns in this town that aren't should be yours and mine.' Todd had made it a non-negotiable condition of his employment that he was exempt from the ban on guns in Morton's Cross.

'Dunno. Let's go and check.' The two men left the theatre and walked across the street to the sheriff's office. Zac looked at the programme for the show and cross-checked everyone in it or associated with it against the gun log.

'Nope,' he said. 'Nothin' registered.'

'Good,' said Todd. 'I'd be grateful if you'd let me handle this incident from here. It potentially creates an advantage

for me in regards what I'm here to do.'
Zac nodded in agreement.

Todd warmed towards Zac Riley. Zac's natural inclination towards distrust of others' motives was a useful quality for a law man, or at least a town-based sheriff. By the same token, McFarlane wouldn't necessarily want to work with Zac in the field. When McFarlane was on a job, he was totally task focused and couldn't afford the distraction from someone whose caution could be driven by emotion, misleadingly masquerading itself as intuition, rather than being rooted in hard, cold fact.

When Todd got back to the theatre, the audience was leaving the building. He fought his way through the exiting throng, bought himself a whiskey and sat down at a table close to one end of the bar. Right on cue at the other end of the bar, Dan McCleery came and stood behind Trixie-Lou Sanders, his right arm around her waist as she leaned against the bar, facing Todd.

Todd tried to catch McCleery's eye in the mirror that ran the length of the wall at the back of the saloon, but to no avail. McCleery was too engrossed in his female companion. Including the barman, they were the only four people in the saloon.

Todd stood up, scraping the chair legs backwards on the floor. The noise attracted McCleery's attention. And as Dan looked up from the nape of Trixie-Lou's neck, he saw McFarlane draw back his coat to reveal a holstered Schofield revolver. Undaunted, McCleery discreetly put his left hand inside his companion's skirts, slowly moving it over Trixie-Lou's left thigh until he felt the small revolver she kept by her garter. He carefully removed the gun from its holster. Unbeknown to McCleery, Todd could see this activity in the mirror.

'If yer not a good shot, mister, I'd drop yer gun. Yer wouldn't wanna shoot this lady in the back by accident, now would yer?' McCleery asked confidently.

'No,' replied McFarlane, 'an' I ain't gonna.' He fired the Schofield as he spoke, winging McCleery's trigger hand. 'Yer see, McCleery, I am a good shot!' McCleery ran out of the back of the theatre. 'I'll come back for him, I'm takin' you to the sheriff's office first,' he said, grabbing hold of Trixie-Lou's wrist, 'for illegal gun smuggling.'

★   ★   ★

By the time Dan got back to the Eagle, McFarlane had made himself scarce; he hadn't bargained on McCleery going anywhere fast because the livery was shut and the next stage out of town wasn't until the morning. But what McFarlane hadn't bargained on either was the two-hour late arrival of the north-bound train. He heard the noise of its whistle as it arrived and raced towards the station but couldn't find McCleery among the crowd. He searched all along the platform as best as he could but there was no sign. It

71

was only as the train pulled out of the station that McCleery became plainly visible. He was standing by the open window in one of the carriages, smiling at McFarlane and waving at him.

'Damn,' Todd muttered to himself. 'This man is going to be quite an adversary.'

He walked back slowly to the sheriff's office, disappointed that he was unable to get his man. McCleery had got away by chance this time and sooner or later his luck would run out. McFarlane was pleased with his consolation prize, however — Miss Trixie-Lou Sanders. It would be interesting to find out what she knew about McCleery. She stared daggers at him from behind the cell bars as he strode into the office.

'He got away then?' Riley asked.

'Yep, 'fraid so,' Todd replied. 'He jumped the delayed train.'

'Hmm,' Trixie-Lou grunted.

'So tell us what yer know about yer boyfriend, Miss Sanders,' Todd demanded.

'Ain't got a lot to say to you, right now, mister,' came the response.

'Maybe not,' McFarlane acknowledged, 'but smugglin' guns into town carries a two-week maximum jail sentence. Yer could negotiate that down if yer tell us what yer know.'

'Don't know a lot. Only met him on the stagecoach into town a week ago.'

'So what attracted a nice girl like you to a varmint like that?' Zac said. 'Infatuation?'

'No,' Trixie-Lou said. 'Infatuation was what attracted him to me. Intrigue was what attracted me to him. He was an intriguing man. How his mind worked, you know? He was certainly intelligent, possibly intellectual. And a rogue — a free spirit. I find that attractive in a man. I hadn't quite worked out whether he was a loveable rogue or not. You interrupted that line of enquiry. I suspect not as I was starting to be able to control him too easily. I don't find that attractive in a man.'

'Did he tell yer anything about his business or his plans?'

'Nothin' that particularly interested me. Said he was lookin' for a partner to go into business using the resources of the land. Mining, farming, forestry, something like that was what I thought he meant.'

'You know how to fire a gun,' Zac commented. 'Where did yer learn that?'

'Right there on the stage, mister. When you've been shootin' a man's hat off his head at close range while turning round, night after night fer the last few years, well, it hones yer eye. So boys, how am I doin'? Have I knocked any days off my sentence yet? If I don't act, I don't earn.' Todd looked Zac directly in the eye as if to say, 'this is my responsibility from here on in'.

'I'm gonna cut you a deal, Miss Sanders, an' yer can take it or leave it but there ain't nothin' else on the table.'

'Go on, then,' Trixie-Lou urged.

'Well, yer can either stay in this cell

for two weeks or help me find Dan McCleery. We have reason to believe that he is actin' against the law. You know how to handle a gun, which is good, 'cos you might need it. I ain't expectin' no picnic. When yer searchin' fer someone yer need to get inside someone's mind. How they see things, how they decide what to do next. Yer might be able to help me do that. So what d'yer say, Miss Sanders, are yer with me?'

'Sounds excitin', mister. I'm with yer. Let's go!'

★   ★   ★

Dan McCleery puffed thoughtfully on his cigarette as he looked across the arid wastes of the Badlands. Within a week of his release from jail, his whole vision of the future had changed. His last five years had been spent in the unstimulating environment of a prison cell and that had narrowed his concept of reality into an imagined one based on anger. It was a warped concept, hell-bent on revenge for his imprisonment, the stealing of his girl and the general humiliation. He had imagined taking his girl back, killing his oppressors, robbing the Morton's Cross bank and ransacking the town. But now, standing on the outside, he saw a different reality to place his trust in. A reality where he could climb out of the cesspit, be treated with respect by the community, looked up to even, and be wealthy and powerful. They were the qualities any woman worth having looked for in a man. A woman such as Trixie-Lou Sanders, for it was she who had changed his vision of reality.

The acid test, he knew, was always going to be meeting Marie again. If he could only have one of those two women, which one would he choose? And having met Marie, the answer was obvious. He was able to see beyond the poor woman's degradation in physical hygiene. He knew that a bath, a change of clothes and a decent meal would change that. But what he couldn't take was the transformation in her personality. The Marie he knew and lusted after was the subservient one, always trying to please and letting her man know that she put him on a pedestal. But that Marie was no longer there. In her place was a new, energized woman, who at the moment was entirely focused on her own needs and not anybody else's. It was no contest under these circumstances; Trixie-Lou won hands down! So that changed Marie Royston's value status as far as Dan was concerned, from runaway lover to bargaining chip, one for which he guessed, Marie's husband Newt, would be prepared to pay a high price.

Dan had to admit to himself that he secretly admired Newt. He was the sort of man that Dan wanted to be and could have been if he had taken a different turn in the road. The important thing that Dan had realized, however, in the last week was that it wasn't too late to rediscover that turn in the road. In fact, he was almost there. All he needed was one more piece of information! The next morning, Dan told his men not to serve Marie breakfast because he would take it to her himself. The new self-confident, assertive Marie allowed him to enter her prison. He put her food down on the stool and bolted the door behind him. Although psychologically stronger than her guard, unfortunately Marie was not physically stronger. McCleery ripped her dress from her shoulders.

'Now, my little poppet,' he whispered menacingly. 'Tell me all you know about your husband's escarpment and the gold that was found there!'

6

'So what does the note say?' Dwight Farney asked the preacher. The preacher took the note from his pocket. He looked anguished as he started to read out loud the content.

'We are holding Marie Royston. We want to give her back but need to talk with a representative from Morton's Cross who is empowered to negotiate a trade. We have deliberated who would be suitable and have chosen you, Preacher, as the person we wish to conduct our business through. You must, however, come alone. We are not prepared to deal with anybody else or you, if you are accompanied by anyone. Any sign that you are being followed will result in an immediate cessation of negotiations. Tomorrow, you are to take the morning stagecoach west from Morton's Cross and ask the driver to let you off at the Cinnamon Pass. There you are to wait. Someone will eventually come to pick you up.

'By the way, you have been chosen because we believe you have the following qualities: you are sensible and cautious enough not to try any heroics and will warn anyone else against doing the same; you are a reasonable man who will see the merit in our demands and able to portray them to others; you are a mediator and able to take a neutral/facilitation role in order to speed through negotiations.'

'And that's it?' Dwight enquired.

'Yep,' replied the preacher. 'What do yer all wan' me to do? Go ahead?'

'Of course,' said Newt Royston. 'Thank God they've made contact, so that I can get Marie back. You must ask to see her. Check her state of well being. Don't attempt to agree or disagree with any demands they make. You must make it clear that you are not empowered to do that. You have to bring every request back to Morton's Cross for clearance before you can share our stance. That will buy you time, McFarlane, to work out what you're gonna do an' get on an' do it.'

Todd McFarlane stared at Royston. Without taking his eyes off this potentially impatient and volatile man he started talking. 'Where is this Cinnamon Pass?' he asked calmly.

'It's just an entry point into the Badlands.' It was Abe Staunton who chose to answer. 'There's nothin' there, just rock and desert. Stage wouldn't normally stop there 'cos no one in their right mind would wanna get off, but the driver would know it, though — '

'Yer could go an' take a look today, McFarlane,' Newt interrupted. 'See where you could hide an' do a stake-out.'

'No point,' Todd McFarlane said.

'What!' Newt exclaimed.

'The whole gang won't turn up there tomorrow and those that do certainly won't bring yer wife with 'em. Besides, they'll be watchin' it already an' might stop negotiations before they've even begun. We need to go along with what they've asked for initially and in the interim try and figure out where in these Badlands exactly they might be holding your wife. In other words, until the preacher returns from his trip tomorrow, we can't get too much further. Does anyone aroun' here know the Badlands so that we can put some sort of map together, however crude?'

'Yes, I do,' said Abe Staunton. 'In the old days, when I was ridin' the pony express, I frequently criss-crossed that area.'

The preacher didn't sleep well that night, worried about the responsibility that the townsfolk had placed on him.

Preaching fire and brimstone from the pulpit, as man's punishment for his sins, was a far easier task than having to walk into the vipers' nest he might find tomorrow. On the one hand he wrestled with this fear, but on the other he realized it was an opportunity to deal with the guilt he felt from failing to protect Marie Royston from her kidnappers that fateful day at the Royston ranch.

Although he thought he might be walking into a high pressure situation, which would be somewhat of an anathema to him, at least he wasn't being asked to make any decisions, in fact, he was being told not to. What frightened him the most, however, was that under stress he could become accusatory. And he knew himself well enough to acknowledge that he found this tendency difficult to conceal. If it occurred and the outlaws took offence, he would have to point out that it was God speaking through him and not the opinions of the people of Morton's

Cross. That night, he prayed the morning would never arrive.

*   *   *

The preacher returned on the evening stagecoach from his ordeal and no sooner had he stepped foot on the street, than he was whisked away to an upstairs room in the local hotel to be greeted by the members of the Security Association. Dwight Farney organized a bottle of whiskey and a glass for the preacher and bade him sit down and tell his tale.

Relieved that it was over, for today at least, the preacher was able to tell his story in an organized way.

'Let me tell you the headlines first and then I will avail you of the detail. First of all, I was blindfolded virtually from the time I was picked up at Cinnamon Pass until the time I was dropped back here. The only period I was not blindfolded was when I was sat in what was probably an old Catholic confession box, but I didn't know where it was or what building it was part of.' Todd looked at Abe Staunton, wondering if he knew where that might be.

'Second, although I didn't see her,' the preacher continued, 'I was allowed a brief conversation with Marie Royston. She claims to be well and sends her love to you, Newt.' Royston looked relieved. 'I thought she sounded in reasonable spirits. She also said that no harm had befallen her.

'Thirdly, there were no ransom demands made. They want me to go back again in two days' time but to bring copies of the partnership contract between Newt and Dwight as regards the town's water supply, and the land grant documentation proving Newt's ownership of the escarpment.' Murmuring broke out around the room. The preacher waited for it to subside before continuing. 'They also wanted you to know why the events that occurred, actually happened. The cuttin' of the town's water supply was carried out partially as a punishment for the five years' incarceration of Dan McCleery. It was also carried out as a reminder to the town not to underestimate the McCleery gang's capability. The burning of part of the Royston ranch was a punishment for Royston stealing McCleery's girl. The kidnap of Marie herself was carried out to focus the town's leaders on the serious need to meet the gang's demands.'

★ ★ ★

Todd walked with Abe and Zac towards the sheriff's office. 'We need a map that we can draw on,' Todd told Abe.

'Zac should have something,' Abe replied.

'Yeah, I've got a map that includes the Badlands but that part is the only part that ain't got anythin' printed on it, 'cos no one's bothered to map it.'

'I can draw on the bits I know,' Abe suggested. 'We used to use either of two routes: north-south and east-west. The bit I dunno is the bit in the middle, the mountains region, so called. Ain't really mountains, jest mesas, buttes and caves.'

'An' is that where yer reckon they took this preacher?' Todd asked.

'Yep, I reckon so,' replied Abe. 'Back in the old days, there were rumours that there was a small Mexican settlement in the area. The people mainly lived in the caves but there was a chapel and one or two other buildings besides. Miners they were, an' soon as it got around that there might be gold up there, the white man descended on the area in droves. But, a bit like Newt's escarpment, there was nothin' there, or leastways nothin' left, so everybody went away again.'

'So, why would McCleery be interested in seein' the documents provin' Newt's ownership of the escarpment an' the partnership agreement with Dwight Farney?' Todd said. 'Yer reckon McCleery's cooked up a prior claim?

Ownership an' control of the town's water supply would make a man very powerful and exceptionally wealthy. Not only that but it would place him on the right side of the law, if his claim's not crooked.'

Abe looked at Zac.

'Yer need to talk to Zac about that, mister,' Abe replied. 'He's got a theory about that.'

'Well?' said Todd, looking at Zac.

'I might be wrong about this,' Zac cautioned, 'but I attended every day of McCleery's trial an' it always struck me as odd that Royston's men were on that escarpment supposedly findin' all this gold when none had been discovered there beforehand, let alone since.'

'Go on,' Todd encouraged.

'Well,' continued Zac. 'I reckon Royston's men were plantin' gold there, not findin' it.'

'Listen to this bit, Todd,' Abe urged.

'I reckon Royston was doin' that to fool Farney,' Zac said, 'an' make out that the escarpment was worth investin' in. Farney wasn't interested in investin' in water, jest gold. Royston had to deceive Farney into investin' an' drillin'. As it turns out, findin' water an' not gold was the best thing that ever happened to Farney. But dependin' on how that partnership agreement was specifically worded as regards gold or water, it could make the partnership illegal.'

'So, if McCleery's aware of this, he asks to check the legal docs an' test their validity,' said Todd, pursuing Zac's thread of logic. 'An' if they are illegal, the partnership between Farney and Royston is automatically dissolved, with Royston sent packin' in disgrace. Then, if he don't want any trouble, up steps a new partner for Dwight Farney, one Mr Dan McCleery. An' he's kidnapped Marie as a bargaining chip to make sure Royston does his bidding. Somethin' along those lines, anyhow.'

'Yer got it, Todd,' said Zac.

'Well, it's plausible,' Todd said. 'The pieces fit with what we know at the moment. So, yer reckon that McCleery's worked this out since his trial? 'Cos otherwise you would have thought he would have raised it then as part of his defence. He could have lied an' claimed that he wasn't stealin' the man's gold but he found it on the ground an' Royston's man stole it from him, which was why McCleery shot him. One person's word against another, difficult to prove either way.'

'If my theory's right, then he must have done,' Zac said. 'He's had a long time to replay the events of that incident over in his mind.'

'Or Marie knows an' he's threatened her, so she's told him,' Abe commented.

'Hey, cowboy!' Trixie-Lou shouted across the street to Todd McFarlane. 'When we leavin' for these Badlands? I'm a free woman in less than two weeks. I don't wanna be stuck out in the middle of nowhere when my time's up, yer know?'

'If yer don't wan' me to have yer

locked up right now, that's a gamble you'll jest have to take. We should be under way in a coupla days' time.'

'Make it soon, cowboy,' Trixie-Lou retorted as she made her way to the saloon. 'I'm itchin' to get out of this one-eyed crazy town!'

Todd smiled to himself. He reckoned this woman was going to be good company on the trip.

★   ★   ★

Todd and Abe sat in Todd's room above the saloon and pondered over the map that Zac had lent them.

'So accordin' to the scale of this map, this Badlands area is approximately 400 square miles. That sound about right?' Todd asked.

'Sure does,' replied Abe. 'But the middle bit — the mountain region, where I reckon the McCleery gang is hidin' out, is more like ten square miles.'

'That's still a big area to search.'

'It is but I think we can probably call on some help to narrow it down.'

'Go on,' Todd said.

'Well, it's called the Badlands fer a good reason. It's difficult to find water and food out there, especially if you're gonna be out there fer days on end. An Injun would be able to do it but most white men couldn't. They don't have the trackin' skills nor the knowledge to read nature's signs. I wouldn't expect the McCleery gang to have that ability. Hell, I ain't even got it meself!'

'I have,' Todd commented. 'I have survived in this type of country for days on end in the past. As a bounty hunter you have to be able to do that. But, if the McCleery gang don't have that ability, how do you think they are managing to survive?'

'They'll be bringing food an' drink in every coupla days or so, or more likely, payin' someone local to bring it in for them. Someone local who knows the area very well. There's still some Mexicans around, yer know. Two small towns on the perimeters of the Badlands — Maryville, nearly forty miles north of the Cinnamon Pass here and Franstown to its west. Some Mex in both of 'em, descendants mainly from the gold mining days. If we can locate them an' their mules, we can follow 'em.'

'Sounds good,' said Todd. 'If McCleery hasn't got the brains to know how to survive in the wild, d'yer think he's got the brains to dissect a legal contract?'

'Naw, but there used to be a lawyer's practice in Franstown. It's several miles north-west of the mountain region. Dunno if it's still there but we could check it out. Was set up years ago, all part of the gold prospectin'. Admittedly there's unlikely to be a big call for lawyers out there but yer never know. I guess McCleery could have hired someone in. Men like him normally count bent lawyers among their friends.'

★   ★   ★

If Zac, Abe and Todd had any doubts regarding their analysis of what Dan McCleery's strategic intent might be, they were dispelled by the preacher on the return from his second spell of negotiations with the McCleery gang.

'I was blindfolded once more at Cinnamon Pass and the meeting took place in this confession box again, so I didn't see anyone or anything. I was not allowed to talk with Marie but they assured me that she is safe and sound. But, you need to brace yerself fer this gentlemen, especially you, Newt, an' you, Dwight, as well, 'cos neither of yer are gonna like what I have to tell yer,' he warned. 'This trip I learned exactly what their demands are, to which you have got three days in which to respond. They are these; firstly, in light of the fact that Newt's claim to the escarpment land is valid but the partnership agreement is void, McCleery demands that Newt Royston sells McCleery the escarpment land and well heads for a dollar. Then

McCleery wants to form a new partnership with Dwight Farney, giving McCleery fifty per cent of the profits from the town's water supply. Farney will be in charge of running the business.'

'What!' screamed Newt Royston. 'What does he mean our partnership agreement is not valid? Of course it's valid!'

'McCleery claims you led Dwight into it through fraudulent activity. According to the contract, Dwight entered into the partnership on the basis that gold had been found which had been deposited on the site from natural causes and as a result, would be entitled to fifty per cent of the profits of whatever additional minerals or natural resources were subsequently found and reclaimable from the land. The issue is that the gold was not deposited there by natural causes, 'cos your men put it there. That is McCleery's contention.'

Abe, Zac and Todd all looked at each other.

'That's crazy,' shouted Newt. 'An' what if I don't agree?'

'McCleery promised that you won't get Marie back in one piece!' the preacher said in as much of a matter of fact tone as he could muster.

'You bastard,' Dwight Farney shouted at Newt Royston. As a man of principle he was deeply wounded by this revelation. 'You deceived me. I went into partnership with you because I thought that you were a man of integrity. I trusted you!'

'C'mon, Dwight! I made you richer than you could have ever imagined. All it cost you was to be the victim of a small white lie!'

'How do I know you haven't short changed me on my share of the profits? How could I look at the books and trust that they haven't been manipulated? This potentially changes everything. I need a lawyer to look at McCleery's claims an' if they are validated, I might wanna take him up on his offer!'

'You are mad, Dwight Farney! Your

greed has warped your brain, made you mad! I'll tell yer exactly what I'm gonna do, while you come to yer senses. I'm gonna double McFarlane here's fee, to bring home my wife and hand McCleery over to the law to be tried on the charges of disruptin' the town's water supply, burnin' down part of my ranch and kidnapping my wife. Yer see, Farney, you an' yer principles. Is doin' deals with outlaws one of yer flamin' principles? 'Cos it ain't one of mine. Now, if McFarlane is unsuccessful in his venture an' you still wanna partner McCleery rather than me, then I will give McCleery my land in return for the safe homecoming of my wife but I warn you, there won't be a drop of drinkable water on it. The choice as to whether that outcome manifests itself or whether you an' I carry on with our partnership as is, will be down to you, Farney. You need to man up an' not live yer life hidin' behind yer principles but grow yerself some balls made of pragmatism an' expediency!'

Next morning at the crack of dawn, three riders mounted their steeds and quietly left town. Todd McFarlane, Abe Staunton and Trixie-Lou Sanders suddenly found themselves in a three-day race against time with a lot of ground to cover and limited time to find their prey. They planned to reach the Cinnamon Pass by mid-morning, where they would stop and make camp, preferring to cross the Badlands under the cover of darkness and avoid the scorching daytime heat.

7

Zac Riley woke up shortly after dawn in a cold sweat. He knew that he wasn't ill — well, not physically at least — he was suffering from stress. So he did what he usually did on the infrequent occasions he felt this psychological pressure and that was to throw himself out of bed and make for the coffee pot. Over that first steaming hot mug of the day, he tried telling himself to pull himself together. Such self-atonement never normally worked and it wasn't working now. Instead he allowed himself to ruminate over the situation, which only made him feel worse. In fact, he felt alone — isolated in the middle of the town. One of his worst nightmares, the breakdown of law and order in Morton's Cross, was potentially about to come true and all because the civic administration of the town was imploding.

The mayor, Dwight Farney, was no longer talking to the wealthiest man in the town, his business partner, Newt Royston. Royston was no doubt sleeping off a bad hangover while the voice of reason, the elder statesman — Abe Staunton, was on his way to the Badlands, with the man of action, Todd McFarlane. The calming influence of the town, the preacher, was starting to accuse all of them of failing in their duty to the people of Morton's Cross — and true as that might be, under the circumstances it was just plain unhelpful.

That left Zac in charge but on his own. At least the 'guns in town' embargo was still in place, which bought him time. But he knew that as soon as people found out about the civic disorder and the disintegration of the normally democratic town decision-making process, then guns or no guns, there would be riots in the town. He needed somehow to put the town into lock down — close the saloons and only allow certain streets to be used to walk the town, at specified times of day. He had a few deputies to police the situation, which might be enough to prevent a riot breaking out but insufficient to stop one once it had started. His paranoiac mood was disturbed by the appearance at his door of Nat Watson.

'I wan' me guns, sheriff,' Nat demanded.

'Why?' Zac enquired.

'Leavin' town, that's why,' Nat replied curtly.

'Why d'yer wanna do that?' Zac asked. 'You helped build this town. There's a good future for you here once we get through this spot of bother. A bright man like yerself needs to put down roots an' realize the benefit from the investment of his time and effort.' Zac couldn't believe where the energy was coming from to find these words, but they continued to flow. 'Can't spend yer life flittin' from place to place, project to project, idea to idea.' As he spoke he felt his tortured soul, soothed by his commitment to act and lead, start to heal.

The poignancy of his speech was not wasted on Nat, either. Zac's words touched his soul as well but, for different reasons, were more like little arrows. Deep down, Nat knew he could be a dilettante, always looking for the next exciting adventure, whether it was physical or intellectual, often not finishing the task in hand, seduced by the prospect of a new glory. Personally, he loved the West because it gave a man the excuse never to face his inner demons. If the going got tough then it was easy to jump a train and ride; the not so tough could still get going but start over, somewhere else.

'This town's either gonna end up with a poisoned water supply or being run by an outlaw!' Nat threw down his challenge. 'Either way, it's gonna end up with a water supply it can't afford; it won't be able to afford to drink it for health reasons or it won't be able to afford to buy it!' Sensing Nat's words might be covering a slight chink in his armour, Zac wasn't going to give up easily.

'Look, Nat,' he said. 'Poor Newt Royston's between a rock and a hard place at the moment. For my money this is gonna be a fight to the death. The death of Morton's Cross or the death of the McCleery gang. An' it ain't gonna last long. By this time next week, I suspect it will all be over an' we'll know what the future holds. That's the time to move on, not now. I need men who can help me defend the town against McCleery, if he gets to us before McFarlane gets to him. Mind you, I gotta lot o' faith in McFarlane sortin' it out for us, but he might need our help. So you got three options, not one. You can leave town now, or you can choose to leave it later, or you can choose not to leave it at all and enjoy the fruits of your labour.'

Nat swallowed hard. It would be a

chance to deal honestly with his inner fears and own them, to stand up for himself rather than pretend his life was one big exciting 'high', when what he was really doing was running from his own shadow.

'But I ain't no gunman,' he said. 'I ain't no fightin' man in that sense of the word. I wrestle with ideas, not bullets.'

'I ain't askin' you to wrestle with bullets,' Zac replied. 'I know that ain't your strength. I wan' you to use yer brain as to how we might be able to defend those well heads against attack from anyone and then not run off and leave me with the idea but to actually build those defences. Hell, it can't be that difficult, can it? Over the centuries, men have come up with all sorts of ingenious ways of defending the keeps of their castles and those well heads are the keep of ours.' There was a silence as Nat weighed up the situation in his mind.

'I'll do it,' he said. 'I'll do it. I'll need labour.'

'Yer can use Royston's men. If he ever sobers up in time, I'll talk him into the sense of it. If not, they'll do as they are told,' Zac answered. 'I'm declaring a state of martial law aroun' here until this is all resolved,' he added, feeling a new sense of optimism. 'One way or the other, Nat, yer ain't gonna regret this, yer know.'

'I think yer right, Zac,' said Nat. 'I think yer right.'

8

Although their original intention had been to travel in the cool of the night, they first needed to find a campsite that ideally offered shade, shelter, a source of water and food and some firewood. The difficulty of finding such a location in this arid country — with its desert landscape punctuated by buttes and mesas — forced them to change their plans. As a result, Todd, Abe and Trixie-Lou ended up moving slowly towards the central mountain area. It was eventually Abe who spotted a fork off the valley path that narrowed and climbed up the side of a mesa. It wasn't so much the fork or the path that caught his attention but the sight of wild grass at the start of the fork, suggesting the presence of water just underneath the surface.

Digging down beneath the grass, they

found a small underground reservoir, sufficient to fill a leather sack they had brought with them. If they kept in the shade as much as possible they probably had enough water to keep them going, once boiled, for twenty-four hours. They tied the sack on to one of their horses and walked the animal to the top of the path.

The lie of the rocks on top of the mesa afforded adequate shelter, particularly once they had improvised a roof across two large rocks with the aid of a sail sheet they had brought with them. Abe lit a fire, while Todd scouted around the vicinity of their campsite but it was Trixie-Lou who found the first source of fresh food. Turning over a rock in order to find somewhere smooth to sit down she found herself staring at a rattlesnake. Todd found her, frozen to the spot, a look of intense fear on her face.

'Don't move,' he whispered. He knew from the single scale over its eye that it was a Mojave, which distinguished it from its cousin, the western diamond-back, that had three scales over its eye. There was another significant difference that wasn't visible to the naked eye; whereas the venom of the diamondback will dissolve a human being's body tissue from the inside, the Mojave's not only does that but systematically shuts down the body at the same time. In other words, if the snake attacked Trixie-Lou, she would probably be dead in under five minutes. In spite of this scary poison that the snake carried, Todd also knew that the reptile would make a tasty meal for them all, especially if served up with sparrow, a small flock of which he had observed by the water source the three of them had uncovered at the bottom of the path.

Todd found a stick with a V-shaped head and, pinning the snake to the ground, he then dropped rocks on its head.

'Run clear!' he shouted to Trixie-Lou, aware that even though the snake was probably dead, it could still bite and move around! When she was clear, he shot the reptile in the head and cut the head off. He then made an incision into its belly with his knife. After stripping the skin off the meat inside, he cut open the gut and removed the intestines. 'These will make good bait, hopefully for something with a little more meat on it,' he said, throwing the edible bits into the pan that Abe had balanced on the hot rocks that enclosed their camp fire.

'Never seen a man do that before,' exclaimed Abe. 'Get that wrong an' you could be a dead man almost instantly.'

'I've had plenty of practice,' replied Todd. 'Spent most of my life in the wild, yer know. Occupational hazard. Yer jest gotta know what yer doin' an' be mighty careful doin' it. If you ain't experienced then yer'd best stick to somethin' safer like shootin' those sparrows down there,' he said, offering Trixie-Lou his rifle.

'Huh,' she grunted. 'Easier to throw

what little food we brought with us into the open, ain't it, and wait for the vultures to come? They're easier to hit.'

'True, they're easier to hit, but they take more preparation and cooking,' Todd pointed out. 'The problem is they eat carrion and therefore contain parasites. Don't taste too good, either. The trick is to hang on to what we brought with us for as long as possible in case we get caught in a place where it's difficult to find food. Otherwise, we should live off the land all the while we can. The best way to survive in the wilderness is first to gather foods that can't run, such as nuts and berries, then go after stuff that can't run far, like insects, then go for the foods that can no longer run 'cos you've caught them in your traps and snares. Hunting after stuff that runs far and fast can take up a lot of time and effort with no guarantee of success, which can be fatal if your food stocks are low.'

'I get it,' said Trixie-Lou. 'So today's basic menu is sparrow an' the chef's special is rattlesnake.' She took aim with the Winchester and pulled the trigger. 'I got one!' she shouted. 'I hit one! First shot as well!'

* * *

'I've been thinkin',' said Todd as he washed the remains of the sparrow snake stew down with some black coffee. 'This is our first day an' we've got two left to find the McCleery gang before their ultimatum runs out.'

'Go on,' said Abe. 'What's troublin' yer?'

'Well, like you said, McCleery's either havin' his supplies brought in by someone who knows this area like the back of their hand or providin' for himself. If it is the former, then I'm wonderin' if it would be quicker to go and find them and persuade them to show us the way in to McCleery's lair, than wastin' time tryin' to find it ourselves.'

'Well,' said Abe, 'we're pretty sure

111

that McCleery must have used a lawyer to review the partnership and the land purchase contracts, but the only lawyer's practice out here, as far as I'm aware was, an' maybe still is, in Franstown.'

'So the big question is, is it quicker to ride to Franstown and hopefully find someone who can show us or tell us the way into the centre of that mountainous area, or is it quicker to try and find it ourselves?' Todd asked.

'You're worried we'll miss the McCleery ultimatum, ain't' yer, Todd?' said Trixie-Lou. 'And what if we do? What d'yer think will happen next?'

'Either way, whether Newt Royston agrees to his demands or not, I reckon Dan McCleery will ride to Morton's Cross. He'll be wantin' to get his hands on that water supply if Royston's given in to his demands or destroy the place if not. Whatever McCleery's motive, I need to be there to stop him.'

'OK, I've got a suggestion to make,' said Abe, although from the note of satisfaction in his voice it sounded more like he was about to declare a solution. 'It's mid-afternoon. If we give it an hour or so to start gettin' cooler and in the few remaining hours before sundown, why don't we explore if there is a route to McCleery's lair, from the south-east side here? Then if not, tomorrow we'll explore from the south-west. If we're still unsuccessful then on the third day, you go to Franstown while Trixie-Lou and I can explore the north side and try and find a way in from there.'

'Sounds good to me,' said Todd. 'It looks way too difficult to find your way through in the dark. So if McCleery's comin' to town, I don't reckon he's gonna ride until sunrise on the fourth day.'

'Sounds good to me, too,' said Trixie-Lou.

9

'Zac! Zac!'

Riley looked up from his desk as the preacher burst into his office.

'What's up, Preacher?' Zac asked.

'It's Royston. Totally drunk again. Comatose. I'm supposed to travel to the Pass tomorrow to meet McCleery and his gang, hopefully for the last time. But I've got nothin' to tell 'em. Can't even get a word out of Royston regards what I should say, let alone a word of sense.'

'I could bring him in here,' Zac said. 'Throw him in the slammer until he sobers up.'

'I've got to leave first thing in the morning. I need an answer as to what Royston intends to do.'

'An' if yer tell 'em you don't have one?'

'Then that would probably be the

end for Marie and myself. But don't think for a moment that McCleery will walk away under those circumstances. 'Cos he won't. He'll come back an' attack that water supply. The whole town will be dry or poisoned within a few days!'

'An if yer didn't turn up at all?'

'Same outcome but at least I would still be alive.'

'So it's simple,' Zac said. 'You go an' you lie. Sorry, Preacher, you tell what you understand Newt's intent to be. An' that is that he'll sign his land over.'

'But he won't,' the preacher disputed. 'I don't believe he will do that for a moment. He'll wanna fight.'

'He still can,' Zac replied. 'He either fights once he's signed over his land or before. It doesn't make much difference except, if McCleery thinks he's gonna get the land legally, it buys us more time to prepare for the fight. And we are assuming, of course, that McFarlane can't sort it all out before we reach the fighting stage, but we need to prepare for the worst.'

'I guess you're right, Zac. I might be a preacher but under the circumstances, I've got no compunction about lying. What shall we do about Royston?'

'I'm gonna bring him in. Sooner or later he's gonna need to sober up. He's no use to himself or anyone else the way he is. If he is as bad as you describe, he ain't gonna be fully compos mentis tonight. Nor tomorrow, come to that. I'm gonna need to wean him off the booze a bit at a time.'

* * *

The preacher opened his eyes slowly. His head throbbed and as he touched the painful part with his hand, he felt a large bump as if he had either fallen against a rock or he had been hit over the head. When his eyes started to focus he saw leaves attached to the bush on his left hand side, inches above his face. He was lying on his back in a ditch. He climbed out slowly, feeling a little dizzy from the midday heat and dehydration. He rummaged around for his water bottle. He found it in the ditch, top off and empty. He didn't recall having drunk any when he got off the stage at Cinnamon Pass a few hours earlier. In fact, he didn't recall anything from a few hours earlier.

He stood up and dusted himself down. He was a few hundred yards from where he normally waited for the McCleery gang to come and take him to their hideout. He looked around for his jacket and his hat. They were both missing. That meant that his watch had gone and he had no money. He realized that he needed to find some shade because he would have a few hours to kill before the stage returned to Morton's Cross and he didn't fancy the prospect of sunstroke.

What had happened, he asked himself? Had the McCleery gang done this? But that didn't make sense. Why would they want to do such a thing? What was in it for them? Or had McFarlane been seen by them? Had he been hanging around at Cinnamon Pass, hoping to catch sight of the gang coming to pick up the preacher, so that he would be able to follow them to their hiding place? That would have been a silly tactic and surely McFarlane wouldn't have been so stupid to take that risk. Or had he simply suffered the misfortune of being jumped by some road bandits? Either way, why had God chosen to do such a thing?

Marie Royston's life was now truly in danger. As for Dan McCleery, he was going to be hopping mad that his offer had effectively been spurned. Would McCleery give them another chance? And if he did, what price was he going to extract from the people of Morton's Cross for their disobedience? Would he believe that there had been no intent of malice or foul play on the part of the Morton's Cross townsfolk and that he, the preacher had been unable to keep the rendezvous as a result of pure misfortune?

One thing that the preacher did know was that God works in mysterious ways. He took some solace from that knowledge and, knowing that there was little else he could do, he decided to spend the afternoon in contemplation and silent prayer.

★   ★   ★

Zac watched Newt Royston, who was lying on a straw mattress inside the town jail, start to stir. Zac had stopped satisfying Newt's craving for whiskey, not least because the broken man had drunk the small supply that Zac kept in his office cabinet for his personal use. The sheriff knew that it could be dangerous to suddenly stop supplying Newt's body with alcohol completely. Instead, he was supporting the addiction with the occasional glass of red wine and watering it down every time he replenished the glass.

'What's goin' on, Riley?' Newt demanded. 'Yer can't keep me locked up here forever, yer know.'

'We're doin' everythin' we can,' Zac replied. 'McFarlane's gone out to the Badlands lookin' fer McCleery an' so has the preacher for that matter. He left early this mornin' to negotiate the sale of yer land to McCleery.'

'What!' exclaimed Royston at the top of his voice. 'I didn't give my permission!'

'Jest calm down, Newt, an' think about it. Then I'll let yer have another drink. Otherwise yer can jest lie there an' beat yer brains out, 'cos they're the only two choices. If the preacher went out an' told McCleery there was no deal, what d'yer think he would have done? I reckon if you'd have been lucky the reply would have come back with a lock of your wife's hair, sayin' think again, an' if you were unlucky, the same message would have come back with one of her fingers! This way there's still no legal commitment, we're jest buyin' time an' keepin' McCleery sweet, that's all. People are doin' what they can, yer know? Young Nat Watson was about to leave town until I talked him out of it. He's up on the escarpment securing the well head from attack by the McCleery gang. Turnin' it into a medieval fortress by all accounts!'

'Oh,' Newt grunted. 'Anyone else? What's that ungrateful bastard Farney doin'?'

'Nothin' at the moment 'cos I haven't given him a role yet. But once I've got you up on yer feet, I will do, I promise yer. He won't be sittin' aroun' on his butt while the rest of us are tryin' to save this town,' Zac assured Newt.

Newt propped himself up and rested his head in his hands. The combination of alcohol and what he had just heard made him feel introverted and withdrawn, the opposite of how he normally behaved, a sure sign of his stress. Yet what Zac had told him gave him hope. People were able to do positive things without his input. After all, he was in no fit position to provide any positive input himself.

'Glad to see the world don't stop, when I'm not aroun',' he joked. 'Can take yerself too seriously sometimes.' He lay back on the bed, reflecting on what he had just said.

'That's the kinda talk, Newt, that's the kinda talk. Here, you've earned yerself a little top up.' Zac poured a little bit of watered down wine into Newt's glass and passed it through the bars of Newt's cell. 'When yer can laugh at yerself, it can be creative. Relieves the hurt in your soul, helps you discover new alternatives.' And Newt knew that was where he needed to be right now. Supporting and nurturing the protection of those who wanted to return his town, his kingdom, to being a peaceful one again. For too long he had allowed his life to be one big ego trip, hell-bent not just on attainment of power but in being the most powerful.

10

'How long d'yer think Todd'll be gone?' Trixie-Lou said. 'That was another fruitless task today. There don't seem to be any way into that fortress where McCleery's hidin' from the north side, either. It's all gonna be down to Todd now. There ain't nothin' we can do except wait. In fact, there ain't nothin' to do out here, period.'

'There ain't nothin' to do in jail, either,' Abe reminded her. 'He should be back by sundown, if not before. Not long to wait now. Anyways, the later he is back, the better. If he can't find no lawyer or no provider of supplies, then he's likely to be back sooner an' that ain't good news, if that's the case. Yer could sing to me.'

'I could do, I guess,' Trixie-Lou replied. 'But sounds like I could be a long time singing before Todd returns.'

'Yer always wan'ed to be an actress?' Abe asked Trixie-Lou, keen to divert her attention, knowing that a bored camp mate can often put everyone else at risk by being careless in terms of their exercise of vigilance.

'Sure have,' said Trixie-Lou. 'Ever since I was a little girl. Always had a propensity towards singin' an' dancin'. I guess I was quite precocious as a little kid. Always wan'ed to be the centre of attention but with four sisters and five brothers, I knew I had to earn that right. An' I did. By entertainin' folk. Hate routine, always have. Guess that's what I find difficult out here; makin' camp, cookin', keepin' watch, that kind o' thing. I'm lucky you guys don't mind doin' that sort of thing.'

'New town, new character, eh?'

'Exactly. For me, it's all about class, style, panache, standing out from the crowd through outstanding perfor- mance. Best of all, it's about experiencing different people's feelings or how you imagine they experience them, stepping into their lives and being them, if only for a brief spell. But in a way, an' I don't know as I've never told anyone this, it's also my Achilles' heel.'

'Oh?'

'Being an actress, I'm always playin' a different role. I can turn into Shakespeare's Juliet or Lady Macbeth in seconds. And as a result, I don't really know the person I really am. I don't really know myself. Which character is the real Trixie-Lou Sanders?'

'I see,' said Abe. 'I guess that's the same fer all of us, in our different ways. A little bit of our true selves sometimes lies buried an' we're afraid to go find it.'

'Exactly,' Trixie-Lou agreed. 'An' I guess partly that's why I am here on this trip. You guys are searchin' for Dan McCleery but I'm as much searchin' for my true self. When I'm stressed I become hysterical and very dependent on others. I can also become very introverted whereas normally I am strong and self-possessed. But on this trip, well, I am having to learn to deal with the seemingly mundane otherwise I won't survive. I am having to learn to search for facts and bake them into my cake along with my emotions. An' yer know what, Abe?'

'What?'

'I think it's workin', or at least startin' to. It's startin' to make me a more complete person. But what about you, Abe? You said it's the same fer everybody in their different ways. Is there a bit of your true self you're still lookin' for?'

'I guess so, Trixie-Lou,' Abe said thoughtfully. 'I've always been a bit of a lone wolf, me. Certainly, since I was a young man. Too old to remember much before that. Quite happy to be on my own with jest my thoughts. Guess that's why I rode the pony express for so many years. In fact, I prefer bein' on my own, if I'm honest. I am one of life's observers. You like experiencing other people's lives by enacting their ways and behaviour while I like observing the

way they live their lives and comment-
ing sometimes on how that impacts the
overall good for everyone else. Guess
that makes me a bit of a philosopher. In
many ways, I'm the opposite of you. I
need to reclaim the emotionality I may
have rejected over the years through
livin' my life the way I had. I don't
mean from a romantic point of view but
in terms of engagin' with life, in the
way that you do an' showin' commitment rather than standing aloof.'

'An' is this trip helpin' you do that?'

'To a degree it must be,' Abe
answered. 'Like you implied, if you
don't face your demons you ain't gonna
survive out here. I don't think I have
been fully tested yet, but I think I am
ready to step up if the situation presents
itself.'

'Good,' Trixie-Lou said. 'And what
about our friend Todd McFarlane? He
seems to have it all, doesn't he? Knows
how to relate to people, but cool and
dispassionate when it comes to situations, and he has a reputation for

making things happen and gettin' them done. Do you think there's a piece of him missing or is he complete?'

'I've met loads of guys like him on my travels. Many of 'em are so focused on achievin' their goals and enjoyin' the resultin' adulation, that I suspect that they've hidden a little part of their true selves away.'

'Oh an' why d'yer say that?'

'Cos not many of 'em have a good woman in tow, not over the long term anyhow, although normally they ain't short of admirers.'

Trixie-Lou burst out laughing. 'That's an interestin' challenge,' she said.

'What?' Abe asked.

'To play the part of Todd McFarlane's girl!

'I guess Todd could be back after sundown,' Trixie-Lou said. Abe sensed she was getting restless again.

'It's quite likely,' said Abe. 'Won't be a problem findin' us with his trackin' skills, though. Anyways, sun's still quite high in the sky so I guess it's only late afternoon.'

'We jest gotta be patient and wait, huh?'

'Ain't yer ever had to play a patient person in your stage career, Trixie-Lou?'

'Nope an' that's 'cos it's not very entertainin' for folk. Never had to sit still on a bunch of rocks for so long, either!'

'Well, it could be worse,' Abe philosophized. 'We are lucky to have ourselves such a good little campsite here, an' it's all thanks to these rocks. Ain't always the case, yer know. We've got a good view of the valley below, an' we're safe in the knowledge that no one can creep up that cliff face behind us and surprise us.'

'Good,' Trixie-Lou said. 'Well, because you've assured me that we're safe up here, I'm gonna pop behind them there rocks an' have a piss.'

'Make yerself at home, why don't yer?' Abe mockingly, chastised her.

Trixie-Lou soon found a position behind the rocks where she could squat comfortably, protected from view on three sides with just her head on view on the fourth side, enabling her to look down the sheer rock face. She pulled down her drawers and started to pee. From her throne of pure sandstone, she could see a dust cloud moving along the valley below. She stopped peeing.

'Hey, Abe!' she shouted.

'What's up? 'D'yer want some paper for yer butt?' he joked. 'No,' came the reply. 'I told yer, I'm just havin' a pee. There's a dust cloud movin' in the valley below. Yer should be able to see it 'round your side shortly.' She started to pee again.

'Got it,' said Abe. He listened closely. He could just make out the sound of the beat of a drum and raucous, out of tune singing. Three figures on horse-back emerged from the dust cloud. 'Mm, I think they might be comin' this way,' he warned Trixie-Lou. 'Stay where you are fer now. Let me see if I can get rid of 'em if they come up here.'

Having finished relieving herself, Trixie-Lou pulled up her drawers and sat down, with her back leaning against the rock face and her knees in the air.

'OK, Abe,' she called back. The singing and the banging of the drum got louder as the three riders stopped at the fork in the path and decided to leave the valley and take the fork that began to climb the gradient towards Abe and Trixie-Lou's small camp.

'Damn,' Abe muttered to himself. 'I was hopin' they'd stay down on the valley floor.'

He sensed trouble. The party sounded as if they were high on alcohol and opium and as they came into view, their gaudy and dishevelled attire did not persuade Abe otherwise.

'Well, looky here, Silas,' the lead singer said to the drummer. 'We have an old timer sat all alone admirin' the view. That's why we came up here, old man, to admire the view.'

Silas dismounted and had trouble

standing upright. He steadied himself and the bent stove pipe hat that was perched in a crooked fashion on his head. Silas's drum ran backwards down the slope. It cluttered into a rock, twenty yards away, where it stopped. He ignored it as if he was totally unaware that he had let it drop to the ground.

'D'yer know the time, mister?' Silas asked in a drunken fashion. 'No? 'Cos I do.'

He pulled a brass pocket watch from the pocket of the crumpled jacket he was wearing. The jacket looked odd and was clearly too small for Silas's lanky frame. He held the watch in front of Abe's face and let it swing backwards and forwards as if trying to hypnotize the old man. Abe held the watch in the palm of his hand to stop it swinging. As he took a look at its unusual face, he realized that it was the preacher's.

'It's six o' clock in the evening,' he said, hoping to cover his surprise. It also dawned on him why the hat and the coat didn't fit their wearer properly. He recognized them as belonging to the preacher as well. 'Where did yer get such finery?' Abe asked, wanting to know what had happened to the preacher.

'I got 'em in exchange from a preacher who was standing all alone at the Cinnamon Pass,' Silas replied.

'In exchange for what?' Abe enquired.

'In exchange for a large bang on the head,' Silas replied, laughing. His two colleagues joined in.

Abe guessed that the preacher must have missed his rendezvous with Dan McCleery. 'Yer should have brought the man of the cloth with yer. They can sing as well,' he said, fishing for what may have become of the preacher.

'True,' said Silas, 'but I hit him rather hard, you see, so we left him asleep under a bush, in a ditch where he wouldn't be spotted and disturbed. Keep the sun off him, you know. He's probably still there.' The three trouba-dours laughed again. 'Anyway, it's time for more singing and dancing. We will sing and you can dance,' Silas told Abe. He walked shakily down the path and retrieved his drum. 'Right. Away we go,' he said and started banging on the drum at random intervals. 'Old man. You are not dancing. You have to dance.' The second singer stayed sat on his horse, withdrew his pistol from its holster and started firing at the ground around Abe, narrowly missing his feet. Abe was forced to hop from foot to foot.

Right, thought Trixie-Lou to herself. I'm gonna have to do somethin' otherwise we're dead meat. I just need to mentally get into role. It didn't take her long — the seductress become murderess was a part she had played on stage, many a time.

'Well, well, well. What have we here,' said Silas, his leering grin revealing a couple of missing teeth. 'Come to me, my beauty, come to me!' Trixie-Lou held out her hand at just below the height of his waist and used her fingers to beckon Silas to come towards her.

'Look, she wants to play my organ, boys!' he exclaimed. 'The great bard always said that music was the food of love!'

He started to unfasten the front of his trousers. Of course, Trixie-Lou had no intention of touching any part of his anatomy, whether normally concealed by this garment or not, but she had every intention of getting close enough to Silas to be able to grab the revolver that he carried in its waist band. Just when it was in reach she put her hand in her pocket and fired the derringer she kept in her garter through the material of her dress, hitting Silas in the stomach. She grabbed his pistol from his belt and shot the second singer, who was still on his horse, in the head. Sidestepping Silas as he lost his balance and fell forward, she shot the lead singer in the chest. It was deathly quiet. The three bullets had silenced the music forever.

'Well done, gal,' said Abe. 'That was some shootin', Miss Trixie-Lou Sanders!'

'Yes, but it's put a hole in one of my favourite dresses. Abe,' she said, 'I think I'm gonna wet myself. I need another piss.' And with that Trixie-Lou left the stone stage and disappeared into her lavatory behind the rocks.

11

Dwight Farney sat in his drawing room and poured himself a glass of whiskey. This was not his normal practice at midday but these were not normal times. For example, he would not normally have sent his wife East to stay with her sister but, given the fate of poor Marie Royston, he was concerned that his good lady, Jane Farney, could also be in the firing line. So of late, with the house to himself at this time of day, he had taken solace in a lunchtime glass. Alcohol he found, if taken in small doses, could aid the process of reflection. Too much, however, would enable the process of rumination eventually leading to depression, which was what he surmised had happened to his partner, or one-time partner, Newt Royston. Royston, of course had far more life-changing pressures on him at this point in time. Besides, Dwight Farney was a strong man, evangelical in his pursuit of right and wrong, principled with very high standards some would say, and Dwight would be the first to agree with them. After all, he was the mayor of Morton's Cross and he figured that a town that was growing so fast would not have benefited as much if it had had someone of a different persuasion in charge.

He was still angry that Newt had deceived him over the gold in order to secure his investment funding on the escarpment. And it was difficult not to keep thinking about it. But, Dwight reasoned, the only purpose of anger as an emotion was to spur one into action: either fight or flight. Yet the only action his anger was spurring him into was to nurse his wounded pride. And that was what was really eating at him. He felt that he, Dwight Farney, the mayor of Morton's Cross, had been publicly humiliated. He knew that he needed to get a grip of himself or he would end up in a spiralling descent of self-pity.

On the other hand, he knew that he had a lot to thank Newt Royston for. Before they had joined together in partnership, Dwight had been comfortable but not wealthy. He still owned the town's one gun store that he had established a number of years back when he first arrived in Morton's Cross. But it was the water supply partnership that made him rich. And it was that wealth that enabled him, in terms of time and resources, to run for the position of mayor; attainment of which he regarded as his greatest achievement. Dwight had decided to stand for mayor on an infrastructure ticket. He sold the electorate on the 'Farney Way', so that Dwight Farney's mission in life was to build sustainable infrastructures that underpinned democracy and facilitated lifestyles based on quality, equality, and material and physical well-being. For example, his gun selling and repair business supported security and law and order, his water supply partnership supported healthy living and people's well-being. In fact, he had even pooh-poohed that he 'may have been' (as he worded it when challenged publicly) interested in mining for gold at one time, because it didn't fit with his infrastructure mantra. Thus, he linked his past, present and future together as if divine providence had decreed that these connections were meant to be. Not only did it energize Dwight but it also energized the electorate, who voted him in with an overwhelming majority.

Yet right now, Dwight Farney felt that he was at a crossroads; in the short term should he break his own rules and pour himself another drink? In the longer term, did he value a life of bitterness and resentment because people wouldn't do things his way, or should he be more empathetic to others and enjoy the ambiguity of life and the alternatives it created?

The appearance of his sheriff, Zac Riley, at his drawing room door, resolved his short term dilemma for him.

'What can I do for you, sheriff?' Dwight asked, withdrawing his hand from the whiskey bottle.

'I've come to ask a favour, Mayor Farney,' Zac replied. 'Nat Watson's been working up the escarpment, tryin' to secure the well heads and the town's water supply against any further attack. I would go myself but I need to go and check the town's defences. No point in askin' Nat. Yer know what he's like with his enthusiasm, he'd tell yer everythin' is great, even if it wasn't. Wondered if you would go for me?'

Dwight thought for a moment. 'Yes. Yes of course,' he said.

He looked at his sheriff. If ever there was an example to the rest of the town in its hour of need it was this man. Most folk regarded Zac Riley as over cautious, always suspecting a conspiracy against law and order. With everyone around him in authority losing their heads, Riley would have argued his corner with some justification but with him temporarily being the 'last man standing' he had more than admirably risen to the occasion. No longer partisan, as he could be in his analysis, Riley had become the only town leader looking at the situation in Morton's Cross objectively and contemplating how the various scenarios could play themselves out. Not only that but he was also the only one pulling the Security Association together and attempting to co-ordinate activity, whether it be that of Nat Watson, Abe Staunton, Todd McFarlane, the preacher, Newt Royston or himself, Dwight Farney. If Dwight was wanting a signal that wasn't from the bottom of a glass as to how he should behave, he had just received it.

'I'll go up there right away,' he said.

★ ★ ★

The top of the Dunston Escarpment was a hive of activity when Dwight arrived. Nat Watson was directing Royston's men to build what looked like a temporary medieval fort. A gantry was being built on stilts around the well head area with outward facing battlements to protect those manning the gantry. Each of the stilts had barbed wire wrapped around it.

'That's to help stop fire arrows landing in the stilts and burning the whole lot down,' Nat pointed out. 'It's not fool-proof but if any aren't deflected by the wire, it should give sufficient time for us to turn the water hoses on and spray water on the fire through the trap doors in the gantry above.'

'First class! Absolutely first class, Nat. You seem to have thought of everything!' Dwight exclaimed enthusiastically.

'Why, thank you, sir,' said Nat, surprised to receive what sounded like genuine praise from Dwight, who he had down as a man more interested in processes than in relationships. 'I've always been interested in medieval military history,' he explained, 'but there's not much of a call for it these days.'

Dwight took his leave and rode back to town. That went well with Nat, he thought to himself. Dwight had always found Nat too flighty for his liking and insufficiently grounded in reality. Normally, he didn't hold back when criticizing Nat. And that was his second eureka moment of the day; he realized that he was often quick to externalize his resentment of the imperfections in life through being too critical of others. People didn't want his projections; if his way was so good they would attempt to imitate it and seek his advice if they were having difficulties. That was where the win-win lay.

'How's it goin' up there?' Zac asked as Dwight dismounted and tied his horse to the hitching rail outside the sheriff's office.

'Very well,' Dwight replied. 'Very well, indeed, but . . . ' He paused for effect. 'You knew there was goin' to be a but somewhere along the line, didn't you?' Dwight grinned at the sheriff. 'But I think that it might be going almost too well.'

'How come?'

'Don't get me wrong, Nat's doin' a grand job and there's no way that we should stop him, but I think the defences might be too strong, impenetrable even. And if they are, you know what that could mean.'

'Sure do,' Zac said. 'McCleery will attack us at our most vulnerable point, which is right here in the middle of this town. I've just been aroun' the town, lookin' at possible defences. There ain't any really apart from the rooftops. But then will we have enough good shooters? Most of 'em will be on Watson's gantry, I guess. If we could push the McCleery gang down to the bottom of the Dunston Escarpment, maybe we could contain 'em down there in the red light district.'

The red light district was on the

north-east side of town, a small enclave bordered by the east-west trail in the south, the north-south trail in the west and surrounded by a large rock face to the east and north. This geography enabled a natural separation of the less civilized part of the town from the more modern part.

'I might be able to secure some heavier artillery, if you think it's appropriate,' Dwight offered. 'I still have all my contacts in the munitions industry.'

'That would be useful, if you can, mayor. If we're gonna be short on men, then efficiency of fire power could be essential,' Zac pointed out.

'And how's my friend Newt comin' along?'

'He's sober most of the time now,' Zac said. 'But I'm still keepin' him locked up. I ain't sure he's ready to keep off the booze just now. It could go any which way for him at the moment. He's either gonna get all his old strength and energy back, or he's gonna become a broken man. I wouldn't like to say which way he's gonna jump. There's still a bit of chemical addiction but it's the mental addiction I am worried about. The body will sort the former out but ultimately only his attitude can sort out the latter. That's normally the more difficult.'

'Can I go an' see him?' Dwight asked. 'I jest wanna tell him I'm sorry for the things I said and I empathize totally with his situation. As far as I'm concerned, we always were partners an' we always will be.'

'If you're gonna be givin' 'im messages like that, mayor, you'd better get in there an' see him straightaway!' Zac said.

12

Franstown looked dead to Todd
McFarlane as he rode down Main
Street. It was fast approaching noon
and the sun beat down mercilessly on
the hard ground as McFarlane's horse
kicked up the dry dust off its surface.
There were only two possibilities,
either it was deserted or, more likely,
everyone was inside keeping out of the
heat. But as his eyes adjusted to the
light, he could see that Main Street
wasn't totally devoid of life. A man was
sat on a rocking chair on the
boardwalk, shaded by the veranda
above. He gave the appearance of
being asleep, oblivious to the world, his
eyes closed, his head rolled to one side
and his body still. But it was only an
appearance. As McFarlane rode past,
the man opened an eye slowly. Not
many strangers came to Franstown

these days but those that did normally brought bad news with them. It paid to be cautious. The man studied McFarlane's back as he rode down the street.

He doesn't look like good news, the man thought to himself. Gun fighter, outlaw, bounty hunter. They all looked the same as far as the man was concerned. Whatever they said they wanted, you could bet a nickel to a dime that they were really after something else. Which one of the three was this stranger, he wondered to himself. Sometimes, however, it did bring him in a bit of extra cash.

There wasn't a great call on legal services in these parts these days, not since the gold rush had died, so any extra chargeable work was welcome. It normally involved drawing up legal documents giving title for land, property, goods or services to the document's owner. Non-chargeable services were answering requests such as 'Do you know the way to . . . ' or

'Have you seen a man who fits this description?'

Things had picked up a little lately with the McCleery gang in the area, staying at the old gold mine site. Bit of legal advice and a contract between the local Mexican store and McCleery to provide regular food and drink supplies to the site. All strictly within the parameters of the law, Dan McCleery had stressed, but not to be advertised. 'I get on best with people who respect my right to privacy,' was the way McCleery had put it. And small town lawyer Arnie Maddox was not the type to argue.

Maddox watched as McFarlane started to turn round at the end of the street and ride back again. He closed his eyes and waited somewhat anxiously for the stranger to either ride past or stop and call him. His instinct told him that the stranger's demands were not going to be run of the mill. He sensed this man could be a bounty hunter but seeking advice in return for payment — an unusual combination!

'Hey, mister!' Todd called out. 'You run the legal office here?'

Arnie waved his arms and slowly opened his eyes, trying to look startled.

'Sorry, sir. Yes, sir. Arnie Maddox at your service.' It paid to act humble; strangers in Franstown didn't like being challenged or to feel under threat. 'Come into the office. Just taking forty winks between appointments, you know.' His nervous laughter sounded genuine.

'I'm lookin' for a place to stay,' Todd said, taking off his dusty gloves and slapping them down on the counter.

'Ah, you'll be wantin' the hotel up the street on the other side,' Maddox replied. He felt uneasy about this man and the quicker he got rid of him the better.

'No, I'm lookin' for a different kind of accommodation,' McFarlane continued. 'I understand there used to be a working mine near here. In the middle of the mountains. Some of the old buildings still exist, like the chapel for example. Really difficult to find. Good place to stay if you don't wanna be disturbed. You know of it?' Maddox held McFarlane's eye contact. He wanted to look away but he'd lived a lot of his life around gunslingers and he knew how they operated. If he even as much as glanced away, by the time he looked back he knew he'd be staring down the barrel of a gun.

'I've heard of it,' Maddox said. He didn't want to lie because he was not very good at it. He'd wished his brother had stopped promoting this place among the bad and the ugly. But as his brother was quick to point out, there was no big money in being a lawyer in a two-bit town like Franstown. The money from the practice barely paid the rent. The big money came from renting out Stonehenge, as the locals called it. The Maddox and Maddox legal practice provided the perfect cover for this lucrative letting business.

'Who directed you here to us?' Arnie Maddox asked.

'An old friend of mine,' McFarlane said. 'Tell me, if I wan'ed to stay there for a couple of weeks or so, how would I get on for supplies? Yer know, food and water, that sort of thing.'

Maddox didn't like dealing with these types of enquiry when his brother was out of town. After all, it was his brother's business, not Arnie's, and his brother was much better at dealing with these hard cases. Jake Maddox had, in fact, turned into one himself and although Arnie was glad of a share in the profits from Stonehenge, his temperament made him far more comfortable with, and suitable for, the role of honest small town lawyer. He hated filtering these types of enquiry. It was very difficult second guessing the true motive of a potential customer. Get it wrong and you could end up being shot or facing time in jail.

'I understand there is a daily mule train that does all that for extra cost,' Maddox said.

'Good. Can I go and look at it, see if

it suits my needs?'

'I'm afraid it's in use at the moment.' Maddox continued to stand his ground.

'I know,' said McFarlane. 'My old friend who told me about it is staying there. You probably know him, Dan McCleery.' Maddox didn't know what to say, so he briefly looked away. And when he looked back he found himself staring down the barrel of McFarlane's revolver.

'Like I said, Dan's an old friend of mine. He'll be pleased to see me.' McFarlane pulled back the hammer on his pistol and pointed it at Maddox's head. 'What time does the mule train leave town?'

'About now, mister,' Arnie Maddox said nervously. 'Normally leaves shortly after noon from the general store down the street.'

* * *

Tracking the mule train out to Stonehenge was an easy task for an

154

experienced hunter such as Todd McFarlane. He was more concerned that Arnie Maddox had raised the alarm and sent someone to track him but there was no sign of any pursuit so after half an hour or so he put it out of his mind. After a further half hour, the four-mule train and its two riders turned off the main track and rode across the pebble bed of an old dried up stream and its tributaries towards the mountains. It was a clever point to leave the main trail because the pebbles gave little clue that the riders and their animals had changed direction. McFarlane assumed that was what they had done as he could see them a safe distance ahead, climbing a new trail up the mountain side. Halfway up he noticed that they had stopped. The riders then dismounted and disappeared into the rock face into what he assumed to be some sort of cave. He dismounted himself and made the rest of the journey on foot.

The sun cast its bright light across

his path at the entrance to what he had originally presumed to be a cave but turned out to be a recess in the rock face. He ducked down behind two rocks opposite the recess and peered between them, the sun beating down on his back but with the rocks preventing him from casting a giveaway shadow. The mule train had passed through a raised doorway that appeared to work on a chain pulley system and was starting to work its way down the side of the steep Stonehenge caldera. Once it had cleared the doorway, a Mexican bent down and replaced a triangular rock back into the side wall, concealing a lever that McFarlane assumed to be a brake on the pulley system for raising and lowering the door. The Mexican then passed through the doorway to rejoin his colleagues in the caldera. A clanking, grinding noise accompanied the lowering of the door from its aerial rock scabbard to once again conceal Stonehenge's inner sanctum from prying eyes.

McFarlane emerged from behind the cover of the two rocks and walked to the entrance. The door was made of very thick wood, reinforced with a metal grid. The grid would stop an axe attack and the wood was thick enough to stop a pistol bullet. He pulled on the chain. There was minimal movement as the slack was taken up and the gearing mechanism locked in place. McFarlane removed the stone the Mexican had placed back in the wall. It revealed a sturdy wooden handle that he assumed set and released the lock on the chain gear. He guessed that there must be a similar removable rock on the other side that enabled the handle to be operated from inside the caldera, so the door could be raised to let people out. He contemplated trying to raise the door a fraction but thought better of it in case those inside this mountain fortress were alerted to his presence by the brightness of the sunlight that would stream into the caldera as the door was raised. He had achieved everything he wanted to for now and he knew not to chance his luck by trying to achieve more.

★   ★   ★

An hour away from camp, McFarlane was surprised to see vultures in the distance circling in the air. It was difficult to position exactly where they were relative to the campsite and he became concerned that something untoward, possibly fatal, may have happened to Abe and Trixie-Lou. It took him half an hour's ride to eventually get to the sight of the vultures' interest. Three men lay dead on the ground. There were two horses standing nearby. Tracks on the ground suggested that one horse had been dragging its human cargo across the ground. Hoof marks implied that there had been a third horse that had left the scene. Each man had been shot by just one bullet wound, one man had taken it in the head, one in the chest and the

158

third in the stomach. It looked as if their killer or killers had been shooting to kill. Relieved that the bodies didn't belong to Abe or Trixie-Lou, Todd now started to wonder if they were the men's killers. If it had been an old man and a woman against these three rough looking hombres, then it was pretty remarkable shooting.

13

'Mornin', Newt.' The preacher raised his new hat in acknowledgement of Newt Royston. Royston sat on the side of his bed, his cell door wide open, an unopened bottle of whiskey on the floor, alongside an upturned glass. The sheriff had long left on his morning rounds.

'Hear yer didn't make it yesterday, Preacher,' Newt responded.

''Fraid not,' the preacher replied. 'Sorry about that. Got jumped. Nothin' I could do, yer see. Lucky to be alive, I guess, but the blow on the head didn't kill me, an' neither did the subsequent heat and dehydration.'

'No,' Newt said, holding the bottle of whiskey in his hand. 'Must've taken courage, Preacher, for you to come to see me. We never did see eye to eye, did we? You always findin' some validity in other people's points of view, seekin' to find some foundation on which to build a peaceful compromise, me always lookin' to see who was on my side an' regardin' those who weren't as my enemy. Maybe we should have switched roles, you an' me. As a member of the town council, I should be the one trying to tease out people's reasonableness from them an' you, Preacher, you should be the one passionate about justice. Yet my conscience is clear. Whatever I have done, I always felt I did it with God on my side. Even when I deceived Dwight over the gold, I did it with God on my side, knowing it was the only mechanism available at the time to help achieve a far greater purpose from which this town an' all the people in it could benefit.'

'You did it with your god on your side, you mean.' The preacher had been through too much of late for this man, and was not going to start to pander to his arrogance. Royston was slightly taken aback.

'But I guess, Preacher, yer didn't come to pick a fight with me,' he said. 'I guess you've come to fin' some common ground between us, 'cos that's what you do, ain't it? Well, one thing. We're both men of conscience, ain't we? Mine's driven by passion, yours is driven by searchin' for your soul.'

'Right now, Royston, my passion is driven by the desire to find our god, not yours, not mine, but our god 'cos we can only come through this with Him on our side.'

'That bang on the head you took has put some fire in your belly, Preacher,' Newt observed. 'Good to see. I like it. You are starting to act on your own will. That kind of commitment will be somethin' else we have in common.' He started to open the whiskey bottle.

'But if you drink from that bottle, Royston, you won't be actin' on your own free will. You will be actin' under the control of your addiction to alcohol. Our god needs you on our side; not on the side of your addiction. The people of Morton's Cross need you to lead them in the fight against Dan McCleery, 'cos the McCleery gang are surely comin' to town today an' seein' as you think I'm some kind of expert on findin' people's reasonableness, I can assure you Dan McCleery's ran out yesterday.'

'I dunno if I can do this on my own, Preacher. I need a little help. Yer see, my passion has become like a red mist. I can't see straight for it.'

'An' I guess that's why the sheriff left that bottle there. To test yerself, to see if you were ready to step up.'

'It's hard, Preacher. I'm not totally over the chemical addiction yet, let alone the psychological. Ironic as it may seem right now, this town needs someone less passionate than me. Someone who's not directly involved. Someone who's not driven by their desire for what they regard as justice but someone who's driven by a need to complete a task and achieve a goal. The goal of ridding this town of Dan McCleery forever.'

'You are insightful when you lay off the booze, Royston. An' that man is Todd McFarlane, if you remember. That's why we hired him. Not for passion for a cause, we already have you for that. But for his knowledge, his expertise, his intellect and coolness in their application and focus.'

'But he ain't here, Preacher!' Newt Royston exclaimed. 'We don't know where he damned well is. He could have gone home, be lyin' dead somewhere.' Royston poured some whiskey into the glass.

'Don't drink that stuff, Newt!' the preacher shouted. 'It'll set you off again. People always think that the high they're gonna get is always gonna be better than what it actually turns out to be. So what do they do? Have another drink, then another one. Over time, they end up havin' to drink more to get the same effect. An' it always gets worse the more you have. Brings you down, makes you useless. Need to turn yer attention an' yer imagination to somethin' else rather than hopes of false highs. I've never met a man who has told me that continuous drinkin' actually lived up to his expectation of the marvellous sensations he was gonna experience, let alone exceeded them. The men who have come closest to that, who have got some pleasurable experience from that fire water, are those that have had a couple of glasses and then stopped.'

'So what do you do with all your anger, Preacher?' Newt demanded to know. 'I turn mine into a passionate energy that means I can make things happen, an' fight injustice. On those rare occasions, like now, when those outlets aren't available to me I drink it off. But what about you? What do you do? How do you discharge your anger or don't you get any? Yer don't seem like the type of man who bottles it up inside.'

'I get it, same as any other man,' the preacher confided. 'An' after a fashion,

I do bottle it up. But not in a way that's harmful to myself. That don't fit with my faith. I store it so that I can analyze it. Work out how I can discharge it constructively.'

'An' what if yer can't? If yer have to make a stand?' Royston was enjoying pushing the preacher.

'I jest turn all that energy into will. When it comes to a battle of the wills to underpin yer point, you'll quite often find me the last man standing. If there's any excess left after that, my dreams can take care of it, in my sleep.'

'Hmm.' Newt Royston snorted. 'So you're a man of faith, Preacher. What faith d'yer have that McFarlane is doin' what we are paying him to do?'

'Right now?' the preacher repeated, gathering his thoughts. 'Right now, I have faith that McFarlane has a plan to rescue your wife an' take out at least some of the McCleery gang. My intuition tells me that he's not goin' to let us down and he'll turn up wherever and whenever he's most needed. Until he does, we need you to take charge of our defences. 'Cos only you an' he together can save this town. Your passion for action, an' his coolness in directing that action. Either of you on yer own won't be enough.'

'Huh.' Newt snorted again, raising the glass to his lips.

The preacher's gun fired twice. The first bullet shot the bottom off the glass tumbler just below where Royston was holding it. The second shattered the bottle of whiskey into small pieces lying in their own liquid on the jail house floor. The preacher re-holstered his revolver.

'You're preachin' at me again, ain't yer?' Newt asked, admiring the preacher's ability with a gun. He smiled at the man of the cloth stood in front of him.

'Nope,' replied the preacher. 'I'm jest tellin' yer like it is. So are you an' your god on the same side as me an' mine?'

'Yep, we are,' Newt said, laughing. 'You see, I do have the ability not to always take myself so seriously. I can see another point of view!'

14

'So what we gonna do, boss?' asked the member of the McCleery gang who had been voted by his fellow gang members to approach their unapproachable leader.

'Shudup, why dontcha?' Dan shouted at him. 'When I'm ready to tell yer, I will. Right now, I'm thinkin'.'

The man quietly withdrew, leaving Dan sat on his own behind a rock. The men were concerned. It was unlike Dan to be so withdrawn. The smarter ones among the gang were waiting for the explosion of uncontrolled rage to take hold of their boss. They had seen it before. The spiralling down into emotional, sociopathic behaviour. Paranoia of betrayal was the next symptom, from which no gang member would feel safe. Although a number of the men privately thought it might be safer to assassinate Dan, it was a thought they wouldn't dare to share with each other. But if they didn't then the terror campaign would start. Random but violent. Anyone that McCleery saw in his own mind as a potential rival was likely to be wiped out, without any prior warning. But the final stage that the men feared most was total wipe out. A fear of defeat in McCleery's mind could trigger a final violent rampage against everything and everyone around him. That would be his final philosophical comment on the state of the world: 'You might be able to defeat me but you are as sure as not never going to forget me.'

But McCleery wasn't at that level just yet. Being currently only at the reclusive stage, the downward spiral into total anarchy and mayhem had only just started. There was still time to release the grip of the black and white emotional thinking that had taken a stranglehold on Dan McCleery's brain, if only he could stop it. But the events of the day certainly didn't make it easy for Dan to do that.

There had been some strange happenings. First the preacher had never arrived at the Cinnamon Pass. Then Arnie Maddox had sent a late word via one of the Mexican couriers that there had been a stranger in town claiming to know Dan McCleery and 'takin' an interest in Stonehenge'. A gunman hired by the people of Morton's Cross sent instead of the preacher? Or had the preacher been robbed and killed? Indeed, there were various unscrupulous types roaming the Badlands. Then the Mexican had also reported finding three dead men out in the Badlands. Although their bodies had become the evening meal for a flock of vultures, it was still apparent that the men had been shot and were not the victims of sunstroke and dehydration. Things were not going to plan.

Weighing this information up in his mind, he struggled to find alternative

options. The 'red mist' solution continued to rear its ugly head by appealing
to his baser emotions. He'd had such
great plans as well. Realizing the
illegality of the Royston-Farney contract had given him a potential lever to
negotiate his own partnership with
Royston and would make him a very
rich man. It would come at a price,
however, and that would probably
mean losing Marie. After all, Royston
was highly unlikely to give up part of
his business and his wife as well. But
that didn't matter because waiting in
the wings was the delightful and
delectable Trixie-Lou Sanders — a far
better catch!

But now, McCleery's thoughts were
returning to his original plan: that of
the waste and destruction of Morton's
Cross. Except in this incarnation, he
would ride off with a different woman
at the end of it, along with the deposits
from the safe of the town's bank.
Unless something came up to redefine
the course of events. That thought

calmed him down. He felt the rush, as his powers of rational thinking returned, at least to the degree of being able to formulate a high level plan. He would tell his men that the plan would revert back to the annihilation of Morton's Cross unless events unfolded in such a way as to present a more opportunistic scenario. He drew his gun, came out from behind the rock and stood on the ledge in front of his men, like an actor making a dramatic entrance on the stage, silhouetted in the moonlight.

$$\star \quad \star \quad \star$$

'We'll keep the fire going and let it burn itself out in the morning,' Abe suggested to Todd and Trixie-Lou. 'There's enough wood to keep it goin' until dawn and a hot cup of coffee first thing would be very welcome before we make the ride to Stonehenge. You reckon on leaving before dawn, yer say?'

'Yep,' said Todd. 'It's a clear night, so

there will be plenty of stars to help us find our way, in case we get lost. I didn't get to see inside McCleery's fortress an' it would be good to do that under the cover of darkness. See what our attack options are.'

'Findin' your way by the stars is another of your many talents, is it?' Trixie-Lou said, turning towards Todd.

'That ain't no talent, lady,' Todd replied. 'That took years of learnin' by experience!'

'So when yer gonna give this dangerous livin' up, then?' Trixie-Lou enquired. 'Or do yer like livin' on the edge, whittling down your savings until another contract appears?'

'I like livin' on the edge,' Todd said. 'Can't do this forever, mind. It's a young man's game. Live on yer wits. One day, my reactions will start slowin' down and that's the day a younger, faster man will get the drop on me. Trick is knowin' when that day's likely to arrive an' getting' out beforehand. Known a number of bounty hunters fall foul of that. Tempted by one last job that's gonna be the pension.'

'Too late then, mister,' Trixie-Lou commented. 'Get into that way of thinking and tomorrow never comes.'

'An' what makes you an authority on all of that?' asked Todd.

'Formed part of the plot of a play I appeared in once.'

'Oh, a tragedy, then,' said Abe.

'No, it wasn't actually,' Trixie-Lou said. 'It had a happy endin'. Yer see, the bounty hunter in the play invested most of the big reward money he earned and got himself an additional but steady income fer his trouble.'

'Hmm. Smart,' Todd acknowledged.

'It was a smart play. The villain reminds me in so many ways of Dan McCleery.'

'How exactly?' Todd asked.

'On his good side, a bit of the loveable rogue. Engaging, energetic, confident, charming.'

'And on his dark side?'

'Bullying, intimidating, dangerous.

Need to be in total control, you know, a 'my way or the highway' type.'

'An' if you were not on his side?'

'Evil, vindictive. A violent megalomaniac. Winners and losers — me or you, not me and you.'

'So is that exactly how you see Dan McCleery?' Abe asked.

'Sure do. As regards true, unselfish consideration for other people, he's a non-evolved member of the species.'

'Interestin',' said Todd. 'I don't disagree with you. Mr McCleery's problem is that he hasn't left himself in a negotiating position. His offer to Morton's Cross is black and white, shit or bust, whatever way he's tried to dress it up. As you said, his way or the highway. I think we might well see the worst of Mr Dan McCleery an' we need to be prepared for it!'

* * *

'OK, men. Listen up!'

McCleery looked at their frightened

175

faces in the moonlight. They didn't know what to expect and no doubt found the way he started waving his gun around as he spoke particularly intimidating. But as far as McCleery was concerned, that was all part of the theatrics. Being the type of leader he was, he demanded loyalty through whatever means it took to get it.

'The no show of the preacher yesterday may have been an accident or it may have been disobedience, but now requires us to display our fortitude. So, in the morning at sunrise we ride to Morton's Cross. But our strategic intent has changed. It has reverted back to robbing the bank and destroying the town, unless some event occurs that determines that we should follow a different course of action!'

He paused while he scanned the faces of the members of his gang, which had increased to a dozen men. The older ones showed more concern. Some of them were too long in the tooth for a life on the trail and secretly relished the opportunity of settling down and enjoying a sinecure at the expense of the Morton's Cross Water Utility. Dan had promised them that if his partnership with Royston went ahead, that would be paid for out of Royston's share of the profits. For the younger ones it was different. They relished the excitement of life on the trail. Every day a different town, a different woman, a different dollar. The addictive high of robbing banks and spending the proceeds. They were too young to settle down. McCleery had promised them a one-off payment, again out of Royston's share of the profits. But until then both groups needed each other's strengths to counter their respective weaknesses. And that's what made the McCleery gang a successful one.

'Any questions?' Dan shouted out.

'Any kind of event that you have in mind, boss?' one of the outlaws asked.

'Yep. That Royston will still cut us a deal over the water utility. After all, we still have his wife. But if he doesn't then we tear the place down.'

'What do we do with the woman, boss? Do we bring her with us?'

'No. We leave her locked up here. She'll slow us down. If there's fightin' she might get shot in the crossfire, then we have lost our bargaining lever.' McCleery also realized that if Newt Royston didn't want to deal or was killed in the subsequent fight for the town, then he still had an option of Marie, if he was unable to win over the heart of Trixie-Lou. Dan smiled at his own cleverness. He had first and second choice options all down the line. 'Anythin' else?' he demanded.

The men fell silent.

'OK,' he said, 'we move out at sunrise when the sun hits the heel stone in the centre of the caldera and casts its shadow on the western rock face!'

15

'OK, there's the entrance to McCleery's compound.' Todd McFarlane pointed at the wooden door that had been built into the rock face. 'We need to ride off the path and round the outside face a little further. There's a place we can leave the horses. The noise of the hooves would make too much noise if we tried to ride into the caldera. We'd give ourselves away.'

Abe and Trixie-Lou rode behind Todd to the place he had described. They all dismounted and walked carefully back round the rock face. Although the moonlight had prevented their journey from being masked in total darkness, it had still been slower than expected with the horses refusing to go at a faster pace than the one they felt safe with.

'I know this place,' whispered Abe.

'But I didn't know the entrance to the Mexican village was here. We're near Echo Pass,' he added, with the confidence of a man who was once lost but now had found.

'Here's the door lifting mechanism,' said Todd, removing the triangular rock from the side wall. He pulled the lever and then took up the slack of the chain pulley. 'I'll open it just sufficiently for us to crawl under. Less conspicuous hopefully from the other side. The door looks about wide enough to get a horse through, so if we have to leave in a hurry, all three of us should be able to crawl out at once.' As he pulled down on the chain the heavy door started to rise fairly easily. He left it suspended three feet off the ground and applied the wooden lever to lock it in place. 'Let's go,' he said.

They entered the caldera on a path that ran round the inside edge, spiralling down to the basin at the bottom. The moonlight helped to illuminate the scene but also meant that they had to be careful and stay in the shadows. In the middle of the basin was a rock that had been sculpted into a smaller version of Cleopatra's Needle, about twelve feet high. In front of the northern face of the caldera were three or four buildings that were typical one-storey Mexican dwellings. Adjacent to these were the remains of what were once more elaborate civic buildings including a chapel, presumably where the preacher had been taken during McCleery's attempts at negotiating his way to a fortune. Apart from the odd rusting wagon and a pile of wooden pit props, there were little signs of there having been much mining activity. At the end of the line of buildings was a cell door built into the rock face that Todd assumed to be Marie's cave prison. The horses were tethered in front of that cave, already saddled as if a departure was imminent. Abe counted a dozen of them. A fire burned in front of the chapel and as they watched and waited, men started to appear around the fire and then disperse into small groups and drink coffee.

The darkness started to fade as it became replaced by the increasing expanse of early morning light. And at six o' clock the sun started to rise over the eastern horizon. It was a dramatic sight. It shone through a gap in the eastern rock face and shone like a flashlight across the caldera, hitting the pillar of stone standing in the middle and casting a shadow on the western face of the caldera.

'That's why it's called Stonehenge,' Trixie-Lou muttered to Abe. 'It's a place in England, a circle of huge stone pillars supposedly built by the Druids. On midsummer's day the sun rises and as it hits the heel stone, it casts its light into the circle of stones.'

'You're not jest a good shot, are you?' Abe whispered in reply.

★   ★   ★

'OK, men!' shouted Dan McCleery. 'Mount up an' let's go! Colston! Do the door!'

A man, presumably Colston, climbed an iron ladder that was secured to the western face of the caldera and near to the top, removed a small triangular rock from the wall.

'He's releasing the door mechanism from this side,' Todd said quietly. 'Let's move behind those rocks jest up there.' He pointed to a series of large boulders that lay off the track and against the eastern face. 'They're gonna ride up here. I've got a plan.'

The McCleery gang started to ride up the spiral track around the inside face of the caldera. The horses walked slowly but steadily up the grit-covered path to avoid slipping backwards or, at worst, falling over the edge. From behind their stone shield, Todd, Trixie-Lou and Abe had a good view of the men's faces, serious but sullen; it was difficult to know what was going through their minds. After the twelfth and final man passed, Todd turned to Trixie-Lou and passed his Winchester.

'As the ninth man goes to pass through the doorway, I want you to fire the rifle over his head. Try not to hit him, it's never good form to hit a man in the back,' he said. 'We'll take the last four out as they turn round,' he said to Abe.

Not used to the Winchester, Trixie-Lou found it heavier to lift than she anticipated. Frightened of letting the ninth man pass through the doorway, she hastily pulled the priming lever down and up to load the gun, and squeezed the trigger. The bullet just missed the man's head but blew his hat clean away. The almost comedic nature of the shot caught McCleery's men off guard and the last four men turned slowly, allowing Abe and Todd to choose their body target. All four men fell instantly to the ground as each of their chests were punctured by a hail of bullets. Their horses blocked the gateway.

'Lower the damned door, lower the door!' Dan McCleery barked. He recognized Trixie-Lou as she raised her head above the rock to take aim at him with the Winchester. He ducked back out of the way. Some of his men returned fire as the door was lowered, finally trapping one of the riderless horses inside the cauldron along with Todd, Abe and Trixie-Lou.

'Let's go!' McCleery screamed, absolutely livid. The dream was over. Trixie-Lou had betrayed him and the town of Morton's Cross had defied him. It was time to let the nightmare begin.

'Colston!' The man nervously rode up alongside McCleery. 'How d'yer think those gunmen an' that whore of an actress got in?' he shouted.

'I dunno, boss,' Colston answered.

'Yer dunno? Well, I'll tell yer. Yer didn't shut the damned door properly last night, that's how. You were too damned drunk again!'

'D'yer wan' me to go back an' kill

'em?' Colston offered. He didn't know whether he had shut the door down properly or not last night but he did know that he had been out of his head on rot gut whiskey. He didn't need McCleery to remind him. His splitting headache was a sufficient reminder.

'No, they'll die in there soon enough.' McCleery pointed with some delight. 'There's no food or water left an' they'll never figure out where the lever to open the door from inside the cauldron is concealed. A slow death is what they deserve, not a quick mercy killin'.' McCleery stopped his horse, so Colston did the same. 'Unlike you, Colston,' McCleery added.

He removed his six-shooter from its holster and pointing it at Colston's forehead, pulled the trigger. A spurt of blood squirted from the man's forehead. With a look of terror frozen on his face, Colston fell off his horse and lay dead on the ground. And then there were seven.

'Right men,' McCleery said to his diminished band. 'Let's tear Morton's Cross apart!'

16

'D'yer hear that, boys?' Trixie-Lou asked.

'A single gunshot,' said Abe. 'Strange.'

'Hope they haven't found our horses and fired it to disperse them. Otherwise we've only got that one of theirs.' She pointed at the roan below that was chewing at a tuft of grass on the floor of the caldera. 'No good between three of us.'

'Even worse between four of us,' Todd pointed out. 'Look, that must be Marie Royston waving through the cell door down there.'

'Damn right it is,' said Abe. 'Marie!' he shouted out, waving back. 'We're comin' down to let you out!'

* * *

Marie was overjoyed to see them. Given her ordeal, she looked well enough and was in good spirits. She knew all about Dan's intent to be her husband's partner in his water utility business and how negotiations had stalled. Her captors hadn't tried to keep such talk from her. As far they were concerned she was just a negotiating counter and were only interested in keeping her alive to fulfil that role. Otherwise, mercifully they had left her alone. The gang knew it was not good form to start messing with the boss's 'ex' and had managed to control any desire to do so.

'So what's the plan, Todd?' Trixie-Lou said.

'Well, first we need to get out of here an' check if our horses are still where we left 'em. If so, I wanna hotfoot it to Morton's Cross. If I could get there ahead of the McCleery gang, I could warn the townsfolk that Dan McCleery is coming. But if not, one of us better ride to Franstown and buy some additional horses.'

'Well, getting out of here is easy enough,' Marie said. 'I've watched

McCleery's men do it enough times. The lock for the door pulley mechanism is hidden behind a triangular rock up there,' she said, pointing to the western face of the caldera. 'In fact, I can see it from here.'

'You've got darn good eyesight,' Abe commented.

'I jest know what I'm lookin' for and whereabouts it is,' Marie replied. 'The gang often used to open it at sunrise to familiarize themselves with the position of the triangular piece of rock. At sunrise, the sunlight in the east hits that needle of the rock in the centre of the caldera, creating a long shadow on the western face. The needle point of the shadow rests on that triangular piece of stone.'

'Hmm, clever,' said Todd. 'Let's try it.'

He climbed the iron ladder that was pinned to the rock face and Marie directed him from below to the triangular stone. He removed it from the rock face, placed it on the ledge that formed the end of the spiral pathway and moved the wooden lever. Climbing on to the ledge, he walked the few steps to the doorway and pulled down on the chain. The door started to lift off the ground. Todd walked out of the caldera and round to where he had hidden the horses.

He was surprised to find not only their original three but another four, which must have belonged to the McCleery gang. A horse's sense of being aware that their own kind are nearby must be greater than man's, he reasoned. With the four men they had shot and the horse already in the caldera that meant there was an extra man, as yet unaccounted for. McFarlane worked his way down the path and at the bottom, lying on the main trail, was the body of one of the outlaws — the man called Colston.

'That explains the gunshot we heard,' Trixie-Lou commented as Todd explained to them what he had found. 'Why would he have shot one of his men when they are about to go to war and reduce the size of his army? I guess the man must have been a traitor,' she concluded, attempting to answer her own question.

'That an' Dan McCleery is havin' one of his psychopathic fits,' Marie said. 'I should know, I spent enough time with him in a former life.'

'Go on,' Todd urged Marie, keen to understand how his enemy's mind worked.

'In the frame of mind he's now in, he is totally out of control,' she said. 'Imagine a spoilt kid who can't get their own way. They start not only destroying the other kids' toys but their own as well. Now scale that up; from a delinquent kid throwing a tantrum to that of a fully grown man. A man, who not only has a gun but has a small army of men, all with similar disregard for the law and all too scared to do anything other than carry out their master's bidding. This man is no longer governed by reason. He is governed totally by his emotions that have reduced his thinking ability to that of a feral dog hell bent on destroying everything around him, including himself. And, there you have it — Mr Dan McCleery on a bad day!'

'Told yer so, didn't I, boys?' Trixie-Lou confirmed.

'We need to get goin',' Todd said. 'I suggest you three ride back together. Maybe go via Franstown and then on to Maryville. It's longer but you're unlikely to meet McCleery on the trail if he were to decide to come back. I'll be able to travel faster on my own but I'm going to have my work cut out if I'm goin' to reach Morton's Cross before McCleery.'

'Not if you go via Echo Pass,' Abe said.

'You mentioned that place earlier,' Todd said, curious to know more.

'Yes, it's a short cut. The main trail, which I suspect the McCleery gang will follow 'cos it's easier, goes round the mountains. Echo Pass cuts right through 'em. We would have used it on the pony express but it was a favourite haunt of the Indians in 'em days. You're up high with good vantage points for the last few miles over the main trail. Good place in 'em days for the Indians to attack. An' yer couldn't always tell where the gunfire was comin' from. The sound would reverberate around the rocks, making it very difficult to pinpoint a gunman's position unless you saw the puff of smoke. That's why it's called Echo Pass. But a word of warning. The path is quite treacherous in places, particularly over the last few miles. So if your horse wants to slow down, allow it to do so and navigate its own path. The dangerous bit runs more or less parallel with the main trail but there are a few places to get down on to it. If you can get down to the main trail at that point, it will be quicker.'

'Thanks, Abe,' said Todd. 'I'll give it a try. D'yer reckon I might make Morton's Cross before McCleery?'

'Yes, I reckon so but yer might wanna

take one of their horses. They look fresher, am I right, Marie?'

'Sure are, Abe,' Marie replied. 'None of the gang have gone far from here over the past few days.'

'What about refreshment?' Trixie-Lou asked. 'Did these critters leave us any food and drink?'

'No,' said Marie. 'They took it all with 'em an' left me enough to last me twenty-four hours. It was a last-minute decision on Dan's part but that's when I knew for certain he was prepared to leave me for dead if he had to.'

'So the second twenty-four hours, things would have started to get difficult for yer. That man's a real nasty piece of work,' Todd said.

'Well, not exactly,' Marie corrected him. 'I managed to pilfer and stash away a few extra days' survival rations whenever they let me out at meal times. I buried it in the sand at the back of the cave to keep it cool. There's enough for all of us to get us back to Morton's Cross.'

'Well done, Marie,' Todd exclaimed. 'A fightin' spirit can make the difference between livin' and dyin'. What about you, Abe? You OK to travel back with the ladies and look after 'em?'

'Jest great, Todd. Jest great,' Abe said. 'Yer know, I've never been particularly good aroun' other people. Been a loner all my life, really. That's why I enjoyed ridin' the pony express when I was a young man. But this trip, well, I've discovered a part of myself I never really knew existed an' that's gettin' the emotional high from enjoyin' the company of other people. So am I OK? I'm delighted. This has added years to my life!'

'Good on yer, Abe,' said Todd. 'Well done. Ladies.' Todd raised his hat to say goodbye as he prepared to ride out.

'God speed,' said Marie.

'Take care, Todd,' Trixie-Lou said, voicing her concern.

17

Echo Pass was like a narrow valley carved out of the top of a high ridge, running along the mountain side. Occasionally, the main trail could be seen below in the middle distance. McFarlane's horse was nimble of hoof and indeed fresh, so McFarlane guessed that he was making good time. Now and again he afforded himself the luxury of stopping and scouring the horizon through his telescope. He tied his neckerchief carefully around the length of its barrel to prevent the sunlight glinting off the brass casing and giving away his position to someone below. Otherwise, no one was likely to see him from the main trail; to the naked eye he would have been no more than a speck against a rocky background.

On the other hand, although the

telescope was unable to pick out the facial detail of a traveller on the main trail, he knew it would be powerful enough to display the outlines of a group of riders, or at least the moving dust storm they create, when riding through such countryside. From that perspective, he felt disappointed. He was hoping at some point soon to catch sight of the remaining seven members of the McCleery gang out there in the distance. He could already have missed them, of course, but he thought it unlikely as they must have had less than a half an hour start on him. At some point, however, he was going to have to hit the main trail himself and he needed a rough idea of how much he was in front or behind them.

In the interim, all he could do was push on as fast as possible. Echo Pass was well named. Although the sound of the horse's hooves didn't create a full echo, they made an unusual, slightly eerie reverberation off the surrounding rock face. McFarlane imagined the Indians of old using the pass. Energized by the trance inducing sound of their war drums, which would have been enhanced by the acoustics of the pass, and with various vantage points enabling the Indians to view the main trail from above while protected from the heat of the sun, it meant that the early pioneers crossing the plains with their wagon trains would have quickly ended up as dead meat.

After a while the pass started to descend the side of the mountain. As it did so the main trail came closer, not only in terms of distance but altitude as well, and the floor of the pass became more broken up and uneven. The geography was changing and Todd realized that the pass must be coming to an end. Those last few miles; the treacherous part where the wiser man, as Abe implied, might wish to make his way on to the main trail. He let his horse walk at a pace with which it felt comfortable but even so the creature starting slipping on the smooth angled stone. He decided it might be safer to dismount and give the horse total liberty to pick its path. The animal continued to struggle, however, and Todd realized that they would need to turn round, go back up the incline and from there find a path on to the main trail. He decided to take another look through his telescope before retreating to old ground.

Holding the instrument steady, he started to scan the horizon once more. Nothing, nothing, nothing . . . and there, to his right, coming into his panoramic view was a moving dust cloud. It was difficult to estimate its speed and distance, so in terms of time the wisest move was to buy as much as possible and find the safest position possible, which reinforced the notion of moving further back into Echo Pass. Todd walked, leading the horse by its reins. It wasn't easy so he went on ahead to scout for a suitable site. When he thought he had found one, which was also near a path down to the main trail, he stopped and looked through his telescope again. The dust cloud was now much larger. Through it, he could make out the shapes of seven riders — the McCleery gang! The larger the cloud, the easier it was to judge its distance and speed, and McFarlane estimated he had a maximum of five minutes before they reached his position. The question then was what to do; trying to pick off all seven riders, who were moving at speed. An ordinary firearm was not a viable option and one that potentially put McFarlane at risk. An alternative was to keep quiet and let them pass undisturbed. But that would potentially give away the advantage of being ahead of the McCleery gang.

As it turned out, McFarlane's horse determined the sequence of events. Tired and consequently nervous at finding its own path across the treacherous stones, the animal slipped backwards and fell. McFarlane tried to coax it back on to all fours but to no avail. The horse had broken one of its hind legs. There was nothing McFarlane could do except put the animal out of its misery with a single bullet through the head. And then the acoustics of Echo Pass came into play.

★   ★   ★

'What was that? Did yer hear that?' one of McCleery's men shouted out over the sound of galloping hooves.

'It was the sound of gunfire, wasn't it?' shouted another of the gang members. 'But listen. It don't sound like jest one shot. Sounds like a number of 'em.'

'It's an echo, ain't' it?'

'Where'd it come from?'

'From those rocks at the bottom of that mountain range we're headin' alongside.'

'Yer don't think it was aimed at us, do yer?'

'I dunno,' replied McCleery, starting to get concerned. 'I think we'd better take a look. I gotta be honest but after that whore of an actress and her mates attacked us so unexpectedly, I'm gettin' a bit paranoid about what's goin' on. Let's go see!'

The gang slowed their horses down to a canter and then a walk as they approached the foot of the mountain range. The sound of the gunfire had died away, leaving an eerie silence. McCleery raised his index finger to his lips, thereby indicating to his men that they should refrain from talking loudly. They dismounted and tethered their horses to the remains of what was once an old fencepost. Taking their guns out of their holsters, they started to climb up over the rocks. It wasn't long before they found the path, from which McFarlane had viewed their impending presence.

'Shit, it's a dead horse,' one of the gang whispered.

'Freshly killed as well. The blood on its face is still warm.'

'That's Colston's horse,' McCleery

said. 'I recognize it. That means it's one of those bastards who shot at us as we were leavin' Stonehenge. I bet it's a hired gunman. His horse was lame, so he shot it. He can't be far away. Let's get 'im. We'll make his death a showcase for the people of Morton's Cross.'

* * *

As McCleery whispered his sadistic words, McFarlane eased his way slowly and quietly down the rocks. Once he got to the main trail below and, keeping close to the rock face, he moved towards where the McCleery gang had tethered their horses. A sly smile danced on his lips. Besides taking a horse for himself, should he untie the other six and let them loose in the Badlands? It would certainly slow down the McCleery gang, possibly prevent them from attacking Morton's Cross or at least for now. But with Marie, Trixie-Lou and Abe still in the

Badlands, their lives could come to a rather nasty and unpleasant end if they stumbled upon the McCleery gang aimlessly roaming the landscape looking for revenge.

Choosing the healthiest looking animal for himself, he decided to untie one more. He led the healthy looking one away from the others and mounting it, immediately put it into a full gallop. He pulled out his gun and fired it once into the air. The second untied horse bolted, while the other five were held fast to the fencepost.

'What was that?'

'Damned gunfire again!' McCleery shouted out, done with whispering and stealth. 'Check the horses!' His men scurried down the rock face.

'Two missin', boss. There goes your gunman!' He pointed at the ball of dust that was fast fading into the distance. 'Looks like he's taken your horse, boss. I can see the piebald roamin' around out there.'

'Go an' get it!' McCleery spat out the

words with venom. 'I'll take the piebald. Two of yer will have to double up.'

'That's gonna slow us down, boss. That gunman will get to Morton's Cross before us, warn 'em we're on our way. D'yer wan' me to go after 'im?'

McCleery smirked at the undying loyalty and confidence of his men. This man was never going to catch up with the stolen horse and its rider. After all, it was McCleery's horse, the best one in the herd.

'No, it ain't no race,' he lied. 'The townsfolk will already know we're comin if they found the preacher. Jest don't know when. We still have that element of surprise.'

'But should those with their own horses ride on ahead?' The man didn't really understand McCleery's reasoning.

'Nope. We're a gang. Part of our strength is in numbers,' McCleery said. 'We ride in together, not in dribs and drabs. We'll jest have to ride at the pace of the horse carryin' two men.' McCleery turned away. 'Ain't a problem,' he muttered under his breath.

★ ★ ★

McFarlane slowed down briefly in order to look behind him. Through the telescope he could see that the gang were way back in the distance, no doubt arguing over who was going to have their own horse. He decided therefore to ease up on the pace a little. This was a good horse and still had quite a bit in reserve but it didn't pay to exhaust the creature when it wasn't necessary. Todd had won the race. He had come from behind and he was going to beat the McCleery gang into town by a country mile. That was important. If McFarlane was going to be the general and co-ordinate the defence of the town, he needed time to assess the situation.

First of all, he would need to gauge the mood of the people and their commitment towards him. There was a lot of money resting on this for McFarlane and once a commitment was made, he didn't let people down. But it would have to be on his terms, one of which was that the stronger members of the Security Association were prepared to follow him. Like Newt Royston, in particular. Newt had always been the town's action hero, a position that his ego would not relish being usurped by a stranger. Even if Newt wanted to be a problem, McFarlane would make easy meat of him. He'd just tell Newt that he didn't know exactly what had happened to his wife. That would knock the wind out of his sails. But, if Newt was prepared to be his deputy, then Todd would tell him the truth — that his wife was well and travelling back in the safe company of Abe and Trixie-Lou. As far as Todd was concerned, it was results that counted, not platitudes. If the odd white lie smoothed out some of the bends in the trail, then that was all that mattered. Inspiring a largely civilian fighting force in believing that they could win this impending assault on their way of life was all about leading from the front.

* * *

The slow pace at which the McCleery gang were now forced to travel helped relax the grip of Dan's emotions on his mind. Not entirely, of course, but given McCleery's penchant for bitterness and resentment, and his unforgiving nature, this was not particularly surprising. What was surprising was his positive assessment of the gang's situation, which a less resilient man would consider slightly deluded. Although five men down, McCleery knew that seven men fighting together as a team was easier to manage than twelve unruly men and consequently more likely to achieve results.

Outlaws without brains are often thought of as ruthless killing machines but in many ways they are just gun fodder for the better organized. Nature's way promotes survival of the fittest and when he made his assessment of who was left in the gang, Dan acknowledged that nature had done its work and it was the bravest and most intelligent members who remained. The five he had lost were the natural cowards of the gang, the ones who would pick on selected individuals and intimidate them because they were more than confident of their safety in numbers.

And the *esprit de corps* of the resized gang showed as they rode through the remainder of the Badlands. Their spirits were high, their banter amusing, and their temperaments spoiling for a fight. They were going to war and most of them — including Dan — knew that they weren't really fighting for revenge, as sweet as its taste might be, but for a change in their lifestyles. They were fighting at least for a large increase in their wealth, if not their power and fame as well. Revenge was the emotional trigger — the energizer, as was the anger brought on by perceived injustice and wounded pride. Discharge of those was the psychological prize, but the acquisition of material wealth and all that went with it was the incentive bonus.

With this particular group of men, Dan McCleery knew that he could lead from his preferred position; the back. Experienced, competent and confident men are able to make their own tactical decisions most of the time in battle. They don't need someone out there telling them every move to make. All they want from a leader is someone who can oversee the turning of strategy into action, the occasional directing hand and words of encouragement. And Dan recognized this. His brains and wily analysis were the perfect complement to his six colleagues' intelligent use of brawn.

★ ★ ★

Todd McFarlane could see the outskirts of Morton's Cross in the distance. He was twenty minutes or so away. Time to try to get inside the mind of his opponent, Dan McCleery. What would Todd do if he was McCleery? There were two strategic weaknesses in Morton's Cross and McCleery would definitely be aware of both of them: the sourcing and supply of water and the actual town itself. McCleery would have given up on the idea of Marie still being his hostage and also of being able to impress Trixie-Lou so there was no incentive to play the businessman and try and negotiate his way into the inner sanctum of Morton's Cross. Unless, of course, he intended to abort his pillage if he was offered a partnership in the water utility. After all, this was all about revenge through destruction. So where did he think McCleery would hit?

The town itself was easier to destroy and potentially less secure once the gang had made their way through the security gates that had been set up as part of the gun control policy. And an angry Dan McCleery should have no problem removing the security gate obstacle from his path. The town also had the bank; an opportunity to get rich in the process of destruction.

On the other hand, the water facility was unlikely to be as easy to hit as last time with increased security patrols. If McCleery took control of the facility by force then it could be a negotiating chip to get his partnership but with a fighting force of just seven men that could be difficult to achieve and if he lost some of them in the fighting it would be almost impossible to secure against a counter attack. It may be, Todd thought to himself, that the townsfolk may have put better defences in place while he had been out of town but all in all, if he was Dan McCleery, then the town would have been a better target to hit for a number of reasons.

★   ★   ★

At their current rate of travel, Dan McCleery estimated he and his gang were still about an hour away from Morton's Cross. Time to reflect on how the gang would make their entrance and carry out destroying the place. Clearly the town had to be laid to waste as otherwise McCleery's reputation as a bad man would be seriously undermined and he would have every bounty hunter and young sharpshooter who was wanting to prove himself constantly on his tail. Even the mysterious gunman who had been a thorn in his side for the last twenty-four hours would have fathomed that that was where McCleery would strike first.

But that was what a rational thinking man would assume. And the problem when rational thinking men apply their logic to other peoples' behaviour is that it escapes their notice that other people don't always behave rationally. Dan McCleery would certainly be the first to admit that he didn't do that. And this occasion was no exception. The thought of gunmen coming after him as he got older and slower often haunted him as it did right now. He was still hankering after that partnership, as much for the respectability and security it would give him, as for the wealth. All he needed to do was destroy part of the water supply pipe again and secure that position so it couldn't be repaired until Newt Royston agreed to his partnership. From Dan's experience, if you studied security guard patrols for long enough, you could work out the patterns of their routines. And then you struck. Even if Royston refused his demands, a town full of dehydrated and unwell inhabitants would fall very quickly. Hell, he probably wouldn't need to take the money from the bank, they'd probably give it to him to go away. It might take a few days to declare his hand and put his plan into action but that element of surprise, the waiting, the anticipation and the resultant fear would begin wearing his enemy down before he'd even fired a shot at them!

18

Zac Riley was McFarlane's first port of call when he reached town and Zac filled him in on the town's defence plans, and their state of implementation. He praised Nat Watson's work on making secure the town's water sources and supply pipe.

'It ain't foolproof but it would be damned hard to attack the well heads,' he pointed out. 'The military might succeed eventually but I would defy Dan McCleery or any other two-bit outlaw to have a go. The supply pipe is less secure because of its length obviously, but we have got regular patrols now who are armed with long distance Sharps buffalo rifles. Dwight Farney got 'em through his artillery business.'

'Sounds good,' said Todd, 'but what about the town? I'll reckon that will be his target of choice because it's so difficult to defend.'

'Well, not everyone sees eye to eye, on that,' Zac cautioned. 'About the town being McCleery's choice of target, I mean. Anyways, we've still got our security gates on the four roads, manned by armed guards. We can put shooters on the rooftops as well but in terms of containment we need to force McCleery into the red light district, as it is easier to fence someone in there. If they set the whores' quarter alight, it will be easier thanks to its position in one corner of the crossroads to stop the fire from spreadin'.'

'Agreed, that's a good thought,' Todd acknowledged. 'How many men have we got who can fire a gun in anger, if they have to?'

'I guess about forty odd,' Zac surmised. 'Half of 'em are Royston's men, mind. He wants you to lead everything, though. He's more than happy to be your number two on this occasion.'

Todd smiled a wry smile.

'That's good,' he said. 'D'yer believe him?'

'Yep, Todd. I do,' Zac replied. 'That don't mean to say he'll agree with everythin' you say, but when it comes to callin' the shots, this man is a changed person, I tell yer, since you've been gone but so are a number of other folk aroun' here. And that's a change for the better as well.'

'I need to talk to Newt Royston,' Todd said.

'Then you'll find out fer yerself what I mean.'

'Where do I find him?'

'He'll be in the saloon. But I guarantee you, he won't be drinking alcohol. More as likely, he'll be supping a black coffee,' Zac prophesied.

* * *

'Todd!' Newt Royston got off his bar stool to greet McFarlane warmly. 'Drink?'

'I'll jest have one of those black coffees, like you,' Todd said. Although Newt was trying to keep strong and show good camaraderie, Todd sensed the man's anxiety and tension. He decided to put him out of his agony. 'Your wife,' he said. 'She's alive and well.' Royston gave Todd a large hug.

'You're a trooper, McFarlane,' Newt said, beaming from ear to ear.

'We found her at the McCleery gang's lair as expected. She's unharmed and travelling back via Franstown with Trixie-Lou and Abe. She'll be safe with them, what with Abe's cool brain and Trixie-Lou's hot shootin' ability.'

'You're more than a trooper.' Royston laughed. 'You're the General, that's who you are! And yer know, the only man a Royston will follow is a General!'

'Thank you,' said Todd, knowing that for the Newt Royston of old, that would not have been an easy thing to say. 'I'll make you my Major then, if I'm your General. OK?'

'Yes, sir,' said Royston.

'OK then, Major. Take me up to the escarpment and show me the defences.'

Todd McFarlane was pleasantly surprised at the state of readiness of the men on the Dunston Escarpment. Nat Watson's pièce de résistance, the armoured gantry, was an inspired piece of engineering. Raised on stilts way above head height and protected by barbed wire, the gantry itself could hold twenty men spread out in a long line with plenty of room to house ammunition and load weapons. The battlements had narrow vertical slits for firing through and their surrounds were protected by metal plates just wide enough to cover a standing man. The nearest protective cover for the enemy were the woods, some hundred yards away, and the Sharps rifles would prevent any attacker hoping to throw a stick of dynamite from getting any closer.

'What's that over there?' McFarlane asked, pointing at some wheeled contraption that was hidden under a blanket of sail cloth.

'Now this really will impress you,' Royston said enthusiastically. He pulled back the sail cloth to reveal a Gatling gun mounted on its two-wheeled trailer. 'Not a civil war one, slightly more modern than that and in perfect working order, too. Dwight got it fer us. We are friends again, him an' I,' Newt hastened to add.

'Good,' said Todd, staring at this piece of lethal technology. Ten barrels, firing a continuous stream of up to 400 rounds a minute and all done by an operator cranking a handle. 'Could do with this in the town,' he pointed out.

'Maybe,' said Royston, sensing a challenge. 'But I think McCleery will come here first because of me. He has a personal vendetta against me. I got him put in jail, and I took his lady while he was incarcerated. And he knows he'll find me with my property up here. I'd like to keep it up here, General.'

'OK, Major,' Todd conceded. 'But if things change an' we need it in the town, then I'll wan' it moved.'

'That's OK, General,' Newt concurred. 'We can get it there very quickly, it's downhill all the way.'

19

'So what d'yer think, boss?' Groningen asked Dan McCleery. 'We've been here three days now an' the boys have got a good idea of the shift patterns on the water supply pipe patrols.'

They had set up camp deep in the forest, some three quarters of a mile away from the supply head. Dan had kept close counsel regarding when and how he would make his move. One of the reasons was that he wanted the information about the shift patterns. But there were others; for example, he still hadn't made his mind up where best to attack, the supply pipe or the town. He also reasoned that the uncertainty surrounding the exact time of attack kept his men on their toes but wore the enemy down. He liked Groningen. A new member to the gang and a more intelligent one. Groningen also appeared to show him considerable respect, unlike some of the low life he had ridden with in the past. They had ridden together from the campsite to the edge of the forest opposite the well head. They sat on their horses in the seclusion of a small wooded glade.

'One thing I do know,' McCleery said, 'is that we ain't gonna attack that well head. Too fortified. We'd never make it across the plain from the edge of the wood, certainly not in daylight.'

'What about under the cover of darkness, boss?' Groningen asked.

'Nah,' McCleery drawled. 'Still too risky, I reckon. That gantry must hold more than double the men we've got an' they've probably all got buffalo rifles. What's that?' he said, looking through his telescope.

'Seen somethin' new, boss?'

'Sure have,' McCleery replied. 'Here. Take a look.' He passed the telescope to Groningen. 'Look in the middle of the battlements.'

'Hell!' Groningen exclaimed. 'That's

serious weaponry! As he focused the telescope more, he saw himself staring at a small circle of the ten gun barrels that fired the deadly continuous charge of the Gatling gun. 'We'd all be mowed down before we got halfway across the plain. Trouble is it's behind that armoured screen as well. We could never take it out.' He passed the telescope back to McCleery. McCleery raised it up to his right eye once more, took another look and then put it down. He sat on his horse silently.

'D'yer wanna run through the shift patterns?' Groningen asked. 'There are sufficient time gaps in which to launch an attack on the supply pipe. Problem is, they could change the shift pattern tomorrow but, if we are vigilant, we shouldn't get caught out if they do.'

'You known in Morton's Cross?' McCleery said, not wishing to engage further with Groningen in a conversation about the supply schedules and the information on them of which Groningen had organized the collection.

'Nope,' said Groningen. 'Never been there.'

'Neither has Bracewell,' McCleery said. 'I wan' yer to take him there tonight. Not for long, jest a little look round. You'll have to give up yer guns at the town gates while yer there. I don't think yer'll be there long — won't need to leave yer horses at the livery. I think I've jest hit on a plan but it requires a little reconnaissance first.'

*   ★   ★

It was sometime after dark when Groningen and Bracewell hit Morton's Cross. They were both wanted by the law further east, for different offences but of a sufficiently violent nature to earn their rite of passage into the notorious McCleery gang. Indeed, Groningen was flattered that McCleery had asked him to take charge of this recce and Bracewell was privileged McCleery had selected him as Groningen's partner. This was a chance to earn their colours and neither of them wanted to screw up.

They offered their guns at the town limits and proceeded to ride in via the red light district. Having spent days living rough, Bracewell, as the younger man, felt a stronger temptation to stop and satisfy his base instincts than the more disciplined Groningen. Groningen's resolve and focus held good for both of them, however, and they proceeded into the main town. Their plan was simple enough. They had two places they were really looking for and as soon as they had ridden through the town once and found them, they split up, Groningen heading for the railroad station and Bracewell for Dwight Farney's gun store.

Although there were no trains scheduled to arrive or leave the station at that time of night, Groningen pulled his hat low over his eyes as he rode by. There were always people milling around that area, regardless of the late hour, given that there were one or two saloons nearby and the fact that the station was the centre of the town's telegraph operation. The track split either side of the single platform, which was also a passing point for trains heading in each direction. Just south of the platform, before the split lines rejoined, a couple of stationary cars stood in total darkness on one set of tracks, obviously parked there for the night.

'Mm, that's a bit of luck,' Groningen muttered to himself. He rode round the back of the cars, where he was least likely to be seen, and lit a cheroot. He then felt inside the torn lining of his jacket and removed the single stick of dynamite that he had concealed there. Sucking on his cheroot to increase the heat of its lighted tip, he placed the tip on the end of the fuse, threw the lighted stick under the front car and then galloped as far as he could along the track and away from the town. He flung himself off his horse and dragged the animal down to the ground with him a split second before the loud explosion.

Through the smoke, he could see one of the railcars rise into the air, like a horse rearing up on its hind legs, and land on its side, straddling the two tracks and derailing the second car. He remounted his horse and calmly rode back into town. People rushed past him, some looking agonizingly his way, anticipating that he was going to confirm their worst fears.

'It happened jest after I passed by,' he lied, not wanting to raise suspicion by maintaining silence. 'Didn't see nobody. Coupla rail cars gone up!'

He then made his way to Farney's gun store, just off Main Street. As he rounded the corner, Bracewell already had a lit cheroot in his mouth. Groningen nodded to Bracewell, who proceeded to light his stick of dynamite and throw it at the front of the store. The ammunition that Farney kept there started randomly exploding like a firecracker. They waited in the shadows around the corner until the smoke started to clear and then stepped over the debris of the front of the store and began to rummage for any undamaged stock at the back.

'I gave up a coupla of good Colts at the gate comin' into town,' Bracewell complained.

'Here, take these.' Groningen offered him a couple of Remingtons that he had found. 'Much easier to reload, these. In fact, yer can jest insert a new preloaded chamber, as quick as that.' Bracewell holstered the guns. 'Let's take these as well,' Groningen added, picking up a Winchester and a Sharps rifle.

After they rode out, armed men started to appear in the streets.

'Make your way to the rooftop of your designated building and prepare to take up arms!' Zac Riley shouted. 'We are under attack!'

20

The two explosions triggered by Groningen and Bracewell were heard by Royston's men who were protecting the well heads on the Dunston Escarpment.

'I need a volunteer to ride as fast as possible to Morton's Cross, find out what's happened and report back.'

'I'll go,' Brady volunteered. 'I did a coupla years with the pony express. I can ride fast.'

'Good man!' Newt Royston patted Brady on the back. 'Pick your horse. Take whichever one you want. Ride fast, no heroics. Find out what happened and report back as soon as possible.'

Brady set off down the escarpment at full gallop. The gradient became steeper after the first half mile and he was able to see the outline of the town in the distance, enhanced by the glow from the flames that were rapidly licking their way through the remainder of Farney's gun store. In the distance, he thought he could make out two riders, silhouetted by the light of the fire coming towards him. Brady galloped towards them at full speed.

When he was within a couple of hundred yards of the riders, he slowed down to a canter. Within a hundred yards, he could make out their physiques but after another fifty yards their facial features started to become clear. He noted both men were well armed. He didn't recognize either of them but since the advent of the railroad, there were at times far more strangers in town than there were locals.

'You come from town?' The men rode towards him and stopped alongside him.

'Yes, bit chaotic down there,' Groningen replied. 'Coupla explosions, suddenly out of the blue.'

'Everyone's runnin' around down there in a blind panic,' Bracewell chipped in.

'What happened?' Brady asked, keen to find out as much as possible.'

'Dunno,' Groningen replied. 'We were mindin' our own business, jest lookin' fer a little entertainment, an' suddenly the place erupted. We'd thought we'd get the hell out, an' advise you to do the same, mister. Place ain't safe.'

Then a thought occurred to Brady. These men were well armed and given the apparent commotion, he was surprised that their guns were returned to them so quickly by the town security. Groningen noticed the look of suspicion in Brady's eye. Bracewell saw Brady's hand slowly move over the butt of his gun. But Bracewell was far quicker on the draw and the bullet from his gun entered Brady's mouth and left through the back of his skull before Brady could remove his pistol from its holster.

'Was that gunfire in the distance?' Newt asked Todd.

'Sounded like it,' McFarlane said. 'Jest a single shot. You wonderin' about Brady?'

'Yep, sure am. What if he don't return?'

'How long's he been gone?'

'Quarter of an hour.'

'We give him another half hour, then we decide what to do,' McFarlane said decisively.

'He may have been ridin' too quick an' his horse has gone lame, so he had to shoot it,' Newt reasoned, realizing there could be a more positive interpretation of events.

'There could be lots of valid reasons but if as a result of any one of 'em, Brady don't return in the next half hour, we need to make a decision,' said McFarlane, asserting his authority.

★ ★ ★

'Was that gunfire in the distance, boss?' one of McCleery's men asked him. The gang, still well concealed in the thick of the woods, had moved a mile further down the escarpment and were making their way towards the edge of the woods.

'Sounded like it,' McCleery replied. 'Jest a single shot. You wonderin' about Groningen an' Bracewell?'

'Yes, boss. They should be back shortly. Hope they're OK.'

'We'll find out soon enough,' McCleery said. 'At least the dynamite went off an' it must have done some damage.'

As they reached the edge of the woods, they could see the light of the flames in the distance. And silhouetted against that light the outline of two riders came into view, making their way towards the woods.

'It's Groningen and Bracewell,' the outlaw exclaimed.

★　★　★

Todd McFarlane sat alone in the dark and rolled himself a cigarette. He had purposely detached himself from the other men and their conversation so that he could listen and think. There was no sound of gunfire in the distance that would signify that Morton's Cross was not under attack. Yet Brady had still not returned with the news. It didn't add up. It was as if the two explosions were just a warning shot to soften the townsfolk up before the main attack. That would be in keeping with McCleery's style, McFarlane rationalized. As would using the explosions as a decoy, to fool his enemy into thinking the town was under siege and then to switch the target of his vengeance elsewhere. But surely that target couldn't be the source of the town's water on the Dunstan Escarpment, McFarlane thought. It was too well guarded against seven men and McCleery must have worked that out.

★　★　★

Dan McCleery poked at the dying embers of the campfire in order to prevent it going out and still provide some light and warmth. He didn't say anything but privately he was annoyed that Groningen and Bracewell had shot the rider on the escarpment on their way back from town. It tarnished another wise well-executed mission. But 'tarnished' he considered, was perhaps too generous a word to use under the circumstances. They may unwittingly have put the skids under his entire plan. It was the lack of response from his enemy that he found slightly unnerving.

The only action they had instigated was to send a rider down the escarpment. He guessed that rider had been sent as a messenger to find out what had happened and then report back. Royston and that mystery gunman must have been wondering whether they needed to send reinforcements from the escarpment to bolster the town's defences. But as the rider hadn't returned and now was never going to, they needed to make that decision for themselves without the vital information he would have given them. McCleery wondered if he had misread his enemy's thought processes. Maybe the well heads weren't as well defended as it appeared. Maybe there was nothing behind the gantry; maybe it was a facade. And the Gatling gun. Perhaps that didn't work, either, too old, probably burned out in the civil war. He was concerned he might need more time to work out what to do next.

★   ★   ★

McFarlane knew he had to make a decision and stick with it. The weakest defences lay in the most vulnerable area, and that was the town. If there was a third target, the winner of the battle would win it in the town. He got up off the log he had been sitting on and went and found Royston.

'OK, Newt,' he said. 'Let's move the

Gatling into the town. You stay here and defend off any attack. I'll take the gun. I jest need three men to help me.' Newt Royston readily agreed. It made good sense. After all, no town, then no need for a water supply. And so, within fifteen minutes, four men and a Gatling gun pulled by two horses started making their way down the escarpment. They hadn't gone but fifty yards when it dawned on Todd McFarlane what the third target was!

★　★　★

'Boss, boss!' Groningen tugged at McCleery's shoulder. 'There's movement on the escarpment!' McCleery, who had briefly drifted off, jumped up from his reverie, grabbed hold of his telescope and hurried to the edge of the tree line. He raised the telescope and adjusted its focus.

'Yes,' he said to himself. 'Yes! Look, men!' His gang followed the direction of the telescope. 'There's our first prize.

That Gatling gun. If we capture that, we can protect ourselves while cutting off the town's water supply and use it to attack any of Royston's men that attempt to repair the damage. And that's how a gang of jest seven men can take a town of a few hundred people. When they are tired and dehydrated in a few days' time not only we will be able to walk in and do what we want with the place, but if we're lucky, we will have taken out some of the men currently defending the well heads who come down to attack us, making the well heads vulnerable as well.'

'Great idea, boss!' said Groningen. 'So we could keep the town if we choose to and not destroy it?'

'Maybe we could, Groningen,' McCleery replied, winking at the smart outlaw. 'Maybe we could. Yer know, the man who designed the Gatling gun, Dr Richard Gatling, didn't see it as a weapon of destruction but as a way of speeding up achievin' peace. An' if all goes well, that would be its role in the battle for Morton's Cross. Seven men on their own are only likely to gain control and get people to listen by systematically destroying the place. But with seven men an' a Gatling gun, then people are more likely to listen sooner. Enable us to show our magnanimous side.' The men laughed. 'We'll attack when they're further down the hill; within the range of our guns but out of the range of those buffalo rifles they've got on the top of escarpment.'

★ ★ ★

Todd McFarlane had discovered that he was riding into a trap. He could have kicked himself for not realizing it sooner. After all, the escarpment was the first target that McCleery successfully attacked and only the other week. But there was no turning back. Progress going up the hill would be a lot slower, leaving them more exposed to enemy gunfire.

'Ride as fast as you can!' he shouted to the other three. 'Without lettin' the gun fall over!'

Their only hope if the gang attacked from behind would be to try and outrun them. Otherwise they would be sitting ducks. If only he knew where McCleery's men were hiding, he might be able to stop and turn the Gatling on them. That would be their best option. The outlaws would certainly be using the wooded side as cover. Attacking a Gatling gun from open country would be risky and foolish. Controlling his horse with one hand, he fired a few shots randomly into the woods to see if it prompted any movement or a return volley.

* * *

'Stay as you are, men,' McCleery ordered his gang. 'Don't move a muscle! They're jest tryin' to draw our fire to get a marker on where we are! We'll need to attack them while they're on the move, so before they can slow that gun down, turn it round and point it at us. As soon as they go past us, we'll ride at 'em from behind. We'll quickly catch 'em up, dragging that heavy piece of metal!' The gang was poised ready, waiting for the signal.

'OK! Now, men!' McCleery shouted. Riding at full gallop, they started to gain on the Gatling gun party. It had to be only a matter of time now.

★   ★   ★

Todd McFarlane turned in his saddle and started firing his revolver at the gang of outlaws who were now in hot pursuit. He pulled alongside the riders in charge of the Gatling gun.

'Head for the trees!' he shouted. He knew that if they could make the cover of the trees, they might be able to swing the machine gun around and turn it on the McCleery gang. He and one of the other men attempted to provide covering fire. Once they made the wood, two men detached the horses and attempted to turn the gun around while the other two continued shooting but from the cover of the forest.

'Abandon the gun!' McFarlane called. 'We need to move deeper into the wood!'

The four men rode their horses deeper into the forest, turning round to fire occasionally and slowly spreading out but keeping within whistling distance of each other. They dismounted on McFarlane's signal and regrouped as a light infantry force, awaiting any sign of movement in the trees behind them to indicate that they were being followed.

★ ★ ★

McCleery realized that his prey had probably disappeared by now. He fired off one last round at random into the woods to test for return fire. McFarlane felt a burst of pain in his left forearm as the outlaw's bullet clipped him. He gritted his teeth so as not to make a sound and give away their position. He looked at his arm. It was OK, bleeding slightly but a small graze rather than a puncture. McCleery waited. There was no return fire, no sound. They must have gone so far into the wood it would be risky to go in and try and find them. Anyway, he had got what he wanted — the Gatling gun. Now his small gang could turn into a formidable fighting force. They could attack the water supply pipe first and then the town. With this piece of modern weaponry, he might be able to negotiate himself a partnership in the running of Morton's Cross! He ordered his men to hitch the gun to one of the horses and slowly drag it back to camp. It had been a successful raid. None of the enemy killed but none of his men hurt, either. Bracewell rekindled the camp fire, coffee was brewed, cigarettes rolled and whiskey sipped from flasks.

McCleery looked at the amazement on Groningen's face as he ran his hands over the Gatling. Groningen had never seen one of these close up before. McCleery picked up his coffee mug and strolled over to the gun.

'Where does the ammo go, boss?' Groningen asked.

'In that hopper.' McCleery pointed at the container. 'Don't require bullets on no belt. No breech loadin'. Jest loose metal cartridges, thrown into the hopper. Works by gravity feed so it can be used by unskilled men.'

'There ain't no ammo, boss,' Groningen remarked.

'What! No ammo!' McCleery exclaimed. He checked the hopper himself. 'Damn,' he mumbled. 'They've outwitted me again. The damned gun's useless. If they had time to do that they couldn't have been as deep in the wood as I thought they were!'

21

'If we survive this, we should put up a telegraph wire between the town and the well heads, atop the escarpment,' Zac Riley suggested. 'Our security forces are split between two locations an' havin' to second guess each other.'

'You mean once you've survived it, dontcha?' Todd reminded him. 'Anyway, it's not a problem now we've got Abe back, eh, Abe? The town's original pony express rider? We'll get you one of the best horses, what d'yer say?'

'You mean I be a human telegraph an' run messages between you down here and Newt on top of the escarpment? I'd be delighted, only too willin' to be more involved an' directly help folk out. I'm ready to start straight away.'

'Great, Abe. Gotta message for you

to take right now. Let Newt know that his lovely wife is safe an' well here in town an' that there is an abandoned Gatling gun halfway up the hill in a small clearing in the woods. He probably knows the place. Oh an' tell 'im that Zac an' I have got things under control down here. We reckon that after last night, McCleery will probably move to a safer camp tonight, deeper into the woods, get a good night's rest, an' attack the town tomorrow early, probably at sunrise. Ouch! That hurt!' Todd exclaimed.

'Well, keep your arm still, mister, an' it won't!' Trixie-Lou retorted as she bandaged the wound on his left forearm where he had been winged by one of McCleery's bullets.

'You know what yer doin', dontcha, Trixie-Lou?' Todd teased. 'Where d'yer learn nursin' anyway?'

'Learnt an' practised it many times on stage,' she replied.

'What, accidents happenin' to the cast?'

'Sometimes, but more often the script demanded it. It was already written in,' Trixie-Lou said.

'But that's fiction, ain't it?' Todd asked.

'Mr Todd McFarlane, I only star in authentic drama. Yer should know that by now!'

'I'm only teasin', Trixie-Lou,' McFarlane said.

'Well, there yer go. All done now. You're gonna live!' she teased back. 'Yer can go.'

'Good, thanks. Nat Watson wants to see me over at the saloon. Says he got some ideas he wants to share with me.'

* * *

'What d'yer say, boss?' Groningen asked. 'Shall we blow up the Gatling? We've still got some dynamite sticks left.'

'No,' McCleery replied. 'Save 'em. We might need 'em later. Sides, I don't wanna attract attention to our position.

I think we best move camp before this evenin' as it is. We all need a good night's sleep 'cos at dawn tomorrow we're gonna attack Morton's Cross and raze the place to the ground!' McCleery snarled.

*　　*　　*

Newt Royston reflected on Abe's message from Todd. He felt he owed Todd one. Todd had let him have his way with the Gatling gun without making a fuss and Newt respected that in a man. He felt he wanted to prove to McFarlane that he had earned Newt's respect. It was the way Newt liked to operate with people. A well-intentioned favour should be returned out of respect. He formulated a plan.

*　　*　　*

'Hi, Nat,' Todd greeted the maverick town planner and engineer. 'Great work on the escarpment, I must say. Made my job easier. Can I get yer a whiskey?'

'Thanks, Todd,' Watson replied. 'Yes, I will. I got some ideas I wanna share with yer.'

'Go on,' Todd encouraged.

'It's about the town defences. You may have a different perspective but from a planner's point of view, they're a little woeful. But yer see, I was asked to design a town that encouraged peace and harmony as the key to prosperity. Not a town designed to withstand a siege. In some respects, the old quarter, with its winding streets slowly climbing away from the crossroads to the cliff face at the back, is better suited to that. But there are some saving graces that probably only I know about that can be used to protect both the old and the new towns. I've got some men clearin' that derailed car off the railroad as we speak. Havin' the track operable could be important to us for a number of reasons.'

'Go on,' McFarlane said while paying the bar keep for two shots of whiskey.

'OK Well, here's my idea,' said Watson enthusiastically, keen to have an interested ear.

* * *

Newt led a small group of three riders out of the compound on top of the escarpment, down the slope and into the woods. He was a man on a mission. Secure in the knowledge that his wife was safe and sound, his partnership and friendship with Dwight Farney had been restored and that he and Todd McFarlane could work together, his energy and optimism had returned. But it wasn't quite the Newt of old. Coming to terms with this harrowing experience had produced a more grounded, less volatile Newt, who no longer always felt the need to lead but who was happy to collaborate when appropriate.

'We need to take it easy, don't yer think?' Newt said as they slowed to a walking pace.

'You're right, boss,' one of the three

other riders responded. 'They might still be aroun', hopin' to trap us if we come to collect our gun.'

They rode that way for another half hour or so, barely saying a word so as to reduce signalling their presence. It was a potentially dangerous situation, since McCleery and his men could easily have already heard or seen them and be content to lie in wait.

Newt Royston felt the adrenalin coursing through his veins. He loved this feeling, knowing that something unexpected may be about to happen and his natural instincts, poised to take over, would decide whether to fight or take flight. As a default position, Newt's were programmed to fight.

One of his co-riders signalled that they should dismount. It was a sign that he had spotted something untoward. Newt followed his lead. Through the trees they could see the wisps of smoke from a camp fire. They dropped to the ground and crawled along Indian style. Newt beckoned to the other two riders to do the same and approach the camp from a different angle and make a pincer movement.

As they got closer they espied their prey, the McCleery gang. Newt realized that, in some respects, Dan McCleery had picked a bad spot to make camp. Although his gang could move quickly into open country and see who might be travelling on the shortest route between the town and the well heads, few thick old oaks grew on the edge of the forest; the type with wide trunks behind which a man under fire could hide and protect himself. This made a well-sighted rifle a very efficient weapon. When both his groups were in place with Winchesters at the ready, Newt gave the signal to open fire. He had bargained that the campers would return fire but, if under pressure, would cut and run rather than risk their lives by wasting time trying to blow up the Gatling. His assumptions proved to be correct.

The one standing member fell to the

ground, killed instantly by the shower of bullets. The other six fell to the ground also but driven by natural instinct to do so. Next, both parties started shooting blindly at each other; firing randomly through the undergrowth, a few inches above the ground, hoping to get lucky. Newt didn't like it; it was a lottery as to who would die and who would survive. He gestured to his men to ease up for twenty seconds or so.

'Put your hands up, McCleery!' he shouted. 'You're surrounded.' He lied, hoping that McCleery might swallow the bait and surrender.

★   ★   ★

With his gang now reduced to six men and even more hell bent on revenge, McCleery had other ideas. He didn't fancy dying in a random shootout any more than Newt Royston, so he gambled that Newt just might be bluffing. If he and his men were really surrounded, then he reasoned that he should have been under fire on more sides than just two. But two sides were enough. It was time to get out and get out quickly. He and his men slid backwards on their stomachs out of the camp, keeping their eyes and guns focused on the two directions from which they had come under attack. As they reached the cover of the forest, Groningen and Bracewell indicated that they would provide covering fire while the other four retrieved their horses. The plan worked a treat.

'Got yer, yer bastards!' McCleery exclaimed. 'Thought yer could out fool me again, didn't yer, but it didn't work! You've met your match, Royston!' he shouted out before turning his horse around and riding with his men deep into the forest, feeling like a victor.

'The boss seems pleased,' said Bracewell to Groningen as they rode through the forest together.

'So?' queried Groningen.

'Well, not only did they shoot Harris

but they've got the Gatling and the ammo for it,' Bracewell replied.

'True, but Harris ain't no real loss,' Groningen pointed out in order to reassure his colleague. 'In fact, he'd have been a liability in the thick of a shootout. You gotta know how to cover an' protect your colleagues. He paid the price for bein' casual an' standin' up when there ain't no need to, especially when you've got men huntin' yer down 'cos they wanna kill yer. The boss knows that an' that's why he's pleased. Royston could have had us then if it wasn't for the boss's intuition. An' if he didn't know before, he now knows that he can outwit Royston. As for the Gatling gun, that thing chews up the ammo an' some. Makes a man inefficient with his marksmanship. Thinks he's got enough bullets to spray 'em everywhere. Yer jest keep your head down, that's all. Once that gun runs out of ammo through indiscriminate firin', there ain't any more left in these parts 'cos we blew up the gun store!' Both men laughed out loud. 'An' remember. We put the railroad out of action as well, so they won't be bringing in supplies from outside quickly.'

'I guess you're right,' said Bracewell. 'After all, they might have the machine gun an' a limited supply of ammunition but we've still got at least a dozen sticks of dynamite!'

* * *

'Well, boss,' said one of Newt's men. 'We did it!' He patted the circular barrel housing of the Gatling gun affectionately.

'We sure did!' Newt replied. 'Thanks to all of you. Thanks very much indeed! I wan' yer to take it to town along with its crates of ammunition,' he commanded his men. 'Go up to the compound first. Speak to the men. Abe Staunton's described to them a windy trail to the south side of the escarpment. It offers good cover, so yer won't be seen from the woods if McCleery fancies havin' a go at winning it back.' Royston felt his energy and confidence had come back through winning that small skirmish; one man killed, a machine gun recovered and no losses on his side. The results spoke for themselves.

22

It was sunset by the time Nat Watson's team had moved the derailed car off the track, and the first train operable since the explosion the night before pulled out of Morton's Cross station. It started to wind its way north parallel to the north-south trail through Morton's Cross. The cars were full, mainly with women and children but also most of their menfolk. In fact, it was everyone who lived in the main town apart from any of the males who worked for Newt Royston, who all stayed to guard the well heads. It wasn't the kind of exodus that Todd McFarlane would have normally planned for but when he had listened to Nat Watson's ideas on structural defences and Dwight Farney's willingness to use his network of acquaintances to obtain the necessary materials speedily, it made a lot of sense.

Those departing looked longingly at the red light quarter of Morton's Cross as the train shuffled past, but in a way they wouldn't normally do, fearing that this might be the last time they would see their beloved town in its current form. As the train gathered speed on its journey northwards, their thoughts turned to the various small townships en route, where they would be dropped in groups, optimistically hoping to spend just one night before returning to Morton's Cross the next evening.

Some of the owners, workers and residents of the red light quarter refused to go, in spite of being warned that any gun fighting between the McCleery gang and Messrs Royston, Farney, Staunton, Watson, Riley and McFarlane might occur in their part of town. Their part of town and the attitude of a number of its people were unique, however. The old adobe buildings and narrow back alleyways were the homes and work places of the original settlers of Morton's Cross.

Throughout its history of Indian attack and bombardment during the civil war, the inhabitants had never entirely evacuated the area and their few descendants that remained didn't intend to start now. Given the nature of its main source of income, there was always business to be done with someone. Besides, if the town came under new ownership, they would just have to move their allegiance to the new owners, who undoubtedly would welcome this profitable source of sustainable revenue.

So that was how the sides looked ready to engage in the siege of Morton's Cross. Six men — one of them a gunfighter, the other five able to use a gun if they had to, against six men, all of them professional gunfighters. The first six had wisdom and knowledge on their side and a rugged determination to preserve a civil and democratic way of life. The latter six, one of them (possibly two) very canny, but all of them were hell-bent on destruction and with precious little idea of the concepts of restraint or reasonableness. Both parties had access to similar light artillery in terms of revolvers and rifles but both had access to different forms of more powerful ordnance, i.e. the good guys with their Gatling gun and the bad guys with their dynamite. On the sidelines were the ordinary citizens of Morton's Cross, most of whom had evacuated the town but supported its current regime, while the few who hadn't remained in the red light quarter to protect the business interests they had there and out of self-survival, were prepared to support a new regime if they had to.

* * *

As the sun rose over the horizon, the six remaining members of the McCleery gang rode towards the outskirts of Morton's Cross. They approached from a north-westerly direction, having cut across country from their overnight camp. As they crossed the railroad, they slowed down to a saunter and followed the main trail south to the crossroads, where they stopped.

'Get a load of that!' McCleery exclaimed, pointing at the newest part of town. 'They've virtually surrounded it with barbed wire. At least all the street entrances and exits are boarded up and closed off with the stuff.'

'Damned place looks deserted as well!' Bracewell shouted.

'Ours fer the takin' then!' Groningen added.

'No, it ain't!' It was the voice of a stranger.

McCleery and his men raised their hands to their eyes to shield them from the blinding glare of the early morning sun. On the roof of the town's bank, a man stood nonchalantly nursing a Sharps buffalo rifle. The holster belt, which hung low on his waist, held two six-shooters.

'You're McFarlane, ain't yer?' McCleery asked.

'Yes, McCleery,' the man replied. 'That's me.'

'So what's the deal, McFarlane?' McCleery asked. 'I'm willin' to do business with Royston. If you're his messenger boy, I wan' yer to go an' tell him that!'

'The deal is that there ain't no deal, McCleery!' McFarlane said. 'Well, apart from the one I have with the good people of Morton's Cross. And that is to hand you over to the sheriff, dead or alive, for the kidnap of Marie Royston and destruction to the Royston ranch.'

'An' what if I ain't givin' meself up?' McCleery taunted.

'I guess I'll jest have to come an' get yer,' McFarlane responded, spitting on the ground at the same time. 'Wherever you are!'

'I need time to think about it,' McCleery said. 'Don't we, men?' He looked round at his gang, who nodded and one or two of them also spat on the ground, mimicking McFarlane's action.

'Yer got 'til sundown,' McFarlane

told them. 'After that we're comin' after yer, but I warn yer, I'll probably be handin' yer bodies to the sheriff, dead. If yer wanna live by givin' yerselves up, then yer better come back here but make sure yer carryin' a white flag an' no guns! Otherwise yer come within a coupla hundred yards of the new town an' we'll shoot yer dead.'

'Well, Mr McFarlane,' McCleery said as he wheeled his horse round ready to ride off, 'we'd better go away an' think about your proposition. We'll get back to yer. One way or the other.' He grinned as he touched the brim of his hat, in a form of mock salute.

★ ★ ★

'Yer got any women, bar keep?' one of the outlaws asked. 'I need a woman to go with this rot gut whiskey yer servin'.' Dan McCleery looked up from the deck of cards he held in his hand and stared at the bar keep.

'No,' replied the bar keep. 'The

sportin' ladies all left town. They don't wan' no trouble, yer see. Not from aroun' these parts, they don't understan' the ways of us long standin' residents.' McCleery looked back down at his hand of cards. Whether it was true or not, it was the right answer. He didn't want his men getting drunk and messing with women before a big fight.

'No one wants trouble, bar keep,' McCleery said in agreement. 'Once we've had breakfast we'll be out of yer hair. Are there many of you long standin' people left in town?'

'Jest a few in the back streets of the old quarter, that's all. Those who can't afford to shut up shop an' miss out on any passin' trade or jest got nowhere to go.' Or hedgin' yer bets on who might be runnin' this place, McCleery thought to himself. 'The new town's deserted,' the bar keep added.

★ ★ ★

'How'd it go, Todd?' Zac Riley asked.

'Oh, jest as expected,' Todd McFarlane replied. 'The normal scorn and derision you'd expect from a critter like McCleery.'

'So what do yer think will happen?' Newt Royston chipped in. 'D'yer think we'll see him again or are we gonna have to go after him?'

'Oh, we'll see him again, all right,' Todd said. 'An' a dollar to a dime says it will be tonight after sundown, our deadline. The hook is baited and the fish is after its food. Yer see, that's how McCleery's mind works. There's no way with an ego the size of his that he's gonna allow himself to be hunted down like the sewer rat he really is. He's gonna come back and fight. And we both know the time for shadow boxing is through. It's put up or shut up time. Bullies like McCleery like to pick a fight when it's on their terms an' we both know that's not exactly how it is any more. His bluff has been called but he'll be man enough to rise to the bait.

This will be over by sunrise tomorrow.'

'So how d'yer wan' us to prepare, boss?' Zac Riley said.

'There ain't a lot to do now,' Todd said. 'The main thing is to get boards across as many of the adjoining rooftops as possible. We need to be able to move around the whole of the new town on the rooftops besides the street. Height gives us an advantage of being able to see people coming an' look down on them. We've got the added advantage of a strong moon tonight but we'll be able to keep in the shadows. I suggest our fighting positions are Newt and Abe taking the east side of the street while Zac and I take the west. Dwight and Nat stay at street level with the Gatling. Once the boards are in place, I suggest you all go an' get some rest. Tonight might be a long night. Until then Abe an' me will keep first watch.'

'Coffee, boys?' Trixie-Lou called out as she strode across the street from the hotel with a tray full of mugs and a large coffee pot.

'I thought you'd gone with my Marie to the ranch,' Newt said, quite shocked to see the actress behaving as if she was the heroine of some western play.

'I was goin' to, Newt, but I changed me mind. Woman's privilege, yer know.'

'I sure do,' he said, the tone of resignation in his voice underlining his statement.

'Some gals need a lot of excitement. Besides, all this life experience makes me a better actress. I don't wanna miss out on this opportunity,' Trixie-Lou said, a smile on her face. Newt looked at Todd for support.

'You heard the lady, Newt,' Todd said. Newt knew that was the most support he was going to get. 'In addition to keepin' the coffee pot topped up, Trixie-Lou's gonna be the ammo runner between the Gatling and the store of cartridges in Zac's office.'

★ ★ ★

'Bar keep!' McCleery shouted out, demanding immediate service.

The bar keep came out of his back room.

'What can I do for yer, Mr McCleery?' the bar keep asked.

'I wan' yer to shut the saloon for half an hour. I need a private chat with my colleagues here. The saloon will be safe in my hands. Bring us six bottles of red wine on yer way out,' McCleery demanded. The bar keep rushed off, keen to oblige.

'Right, men. Now listen up!' Dan McCleery ordered. 'I've got a bottle of red wine comin' fer each of yer. Yer can drink it right now or save it an' drink it later. The only condition is that you're ready to fight to the death by sundown tonight. By midnight I want our work here to be over. This ain't gonna be known in the history books as the siege of Morton's Cross as some of the locals are startin' to describe it but the battle for Morton's Cross that is won decisively, by the McCleery gang. Our victory will be marked, either by the town's elders invitin' us to become partners in its water utility business, which right now seems a little unlikely, or the new town bein' razed to the ground, which will effectively destroy the fortune of the whole place, certainly after we have emptied the coffers of the town's bank. Any questions?'

* * *

'So what is the plan, boss?' Bracewell asked. 'Ain't it right that McFarlane's threatened to turn us into dead meat if we venture within 200 yards of the new town? They've got that damn Gatling gun as well.'

'Yeah, an' if up there on the rooftops, they're gonna see us comin',' someone else added.

'OK, men!' McCleery said, having got their attention and their minds working. 'Now get this! It's true that with the barbed wire an' the Gatling they've turned the new town into a bit of a fortress. But let's look at this a little rationally. First, the Gatling gun. True, it can fire 400 rounds per minute an' no one wants to be on the receiving end of that much lead but the gun is difficult to manoeuvre quickly. Make the wrong decision as to where to sight it an' by the time they've tried to reposition it, the gunner has been shot dead an' the Gatling blown up! Not only that but the gun has a limited firing arc. It's great against marauding hordes or crowds but not against individuals who are fleet of foot and moving in the shadows. Secondly, an' think about this, where can you get within 200 yards of the new town and still have cover from the buildings?'

'From behind the railway station?' Groningen suggested.

'An' from here,' Bracewell exclaimed. 'From the edge of the old quarter, the new town is just across the street!'

'Exactly!' McCleery responded in an encouraging voice. 'Exactly. So which one of those locations is the best? Come on. Think about it.' It was best left for Groningen and Bracewell to work this through. Apart from Dan himself, they were the only other natural thinkers in the gang.

'Not the station,' Groningen said.

'And why not?' McCleery demanded.

'Cos you can probably still be seen from the roof of the hotel, the only two-storey building in town.'

'Yer got it!' said McCleery. 'So are there any other advantages of approachin' from the old town?'

'You can lob a stick of dynamite straight across the street and over the barricades,' Bracewell said with an enthusiasm that relished the prospect.

'Exactly!' McCleery said. 'So yer now know how the battle for Morton's Cross is gonna start.'

*   *   *

Nat Watson proved to be a revelation even for those who had known him a long time. Often regarded by his close

274

friends and colleagues as an ideas person with a butterfly mind, when the chips were down and necessity demanded that it be the mother of invention, Nat proved that he could be its father. Not only by coming up with ideas that were creative but were practical as well, and which he could deliver. If the defences he had built around the well head filled people with confidence, then the work he did with the Gatling gun was inspirational.

Realizing its main shortcoming of manoeuvrability and with the help of some of Newt Royston's men, the previous morning he had laid railroad track down the middle of Main Street. Mounted on the track was a hand cart operated by manually pumping a handle fixed to a lever mechanism. Mounted on the hand cart, on a turntable and tripod, was the Gatling gun. Now, not only could it be moved along the street quickly but the turntable gave it a 360 degree firing range and it could be turned through this by the cartridge loader.

But Nat didn't stop there. There were three or four side streets off the east and west sides of Main Street, which although covered with barbed wire at the far ends, were still vulnerable to attack. Nat even laid rail track down these, which were joined to the main track by small wooden turntables. They may not have stood up to regular use but were sufficient to move the gun quickly to a new position in what was likely to be a short battle. Unable to rest during the long afternoon, his mind on fire with new ideas, he even made a couple of dummy cowboys out of old clothes stuffed with straw and armed with a couple of old Henry rifles, to make the McCleery gang feel that they were outnumbered.

* * *

The streets of the red light district were deserted. Word had got out that

Morton's Cross was a town preparing to be put under siege so the potential punters, regular and casual, were giving the place a wide berth. There was the occasional light coming from the odd house where the inhabitants had decided not to move out. Otherwise, an hour after sundown, the only light anyone behaving furtively would wish to avoid was the moonlight. And that ironically had lit up the centre stage of this soon to be theatre of war, the crossroads that separated the old and new towns.

The McCleery gang were able to move through the old quarter with ease and reach the main east-west trail, just twenty yards east of the crossroads. Groningen and Bracewell were at the front with Dan McCleery content to lead from the back, bringing up the rear. Groningen and Bracewell stopped at the end of the street. They looked behind them and signalled to the others to stop as well.

'Do you want me to throw the

explosive?' Groningen whispered to his colleague.

'No,' Bracewell replied confidently. 'I want to do it. This is for me.'

'OK,' Groningen said. 'You're obviously feelin' good. Does it look good over there?'

'I think so,' Bracewell said. 'There's a couple of men up on the roof over there but not only are they lookin' the wrong way, they're only armed with old Henrys! I think I'm going to throw it in their direction. Won't have to step into the moonlight and can make it count — take out a building and some men as well!'

Groningen nodded his agreement and, taking out a stick of dynamite from his bag, passed it to his colleague. Bracewell walked back down the street some twenty yards, lit the fuse and took a run towards the east-west trail, aiming to throw it high into the air to make sure it landed in the centre of the roof of the building and created maximum impact.

Dwight Farney sat behind the Gatling, his right hand resting on the crank handle. A civil war veteran, he was one of the few to have fired the gun at the battle of Petersburg and what with his professional interest in armaments, he was something of an expert on the Gatling. The gun was already positioned at the north end of Main Street and aimed at the old quarter, on McFarlane's recommendation that that was the area an attack was most likely to come from. Dwight had learnt to sit behind one of these formidable weapons waiting for a horde of armed men to appear, so the presence of a lit fuse flying through the night air was manna from heaven for him. Pointing the gun upwards, he started cranking the handle. A five-second burst was enough for one of the thirty odd bullets expended to hit the stick of dynamite. There was a massive explosion that shook the air, the buildings and everything around them.

But Farney didn't stop. Instinctively, he lowered the gun towards the area where he figured the dynamite must have been thrown from and continued turning the handle, and slightly moving the gun from side to side. It was just like the old days. The faster the handle was cranked, the quicker the rate of fire. In inexperienced hands, however, the gun could jam but not in Dwight's hands. At the peak of this twenty-second burst, he reckoned he must have been pumping out closer to the equivalent of 500 rounds a minute or more. The leaden rain went through the barbed wire and the wooden barricade behind it like a knife through butter.

★   ★   ★

'Bracewell!' Groningen cried out. 'I'm hit bad!'

He tried in vain to stem the blood that was pouring out of various wounds in his body. The silence that pervaded after the gun had stopped firing was as shattering psychologically as it was when the Gatling was in full flow. Groningen crawled towards his colleague and friend. But there was no sign of life coming from Bracewell. Not possible with his face having nearly as many holes in it as a sieve behind a blood red mask. Groningen fell by the side of his friend and expelled his last breath.

'Damn!' McCleery muttered under his breath. McFarlane had won the first round of the battle for Morton's Cross while McCleery had lost his two best men. It was now four against six. 'C'mon,' he called out to the three remaining members of his gang. 'Let's take refuge in the alleyways for a bit an' regroup. I reckon they'll come after us so we need to stick together and cover for each other. The tables have turned — individual guerrilla sorties are out. It's united we stand, divided we fall.' The remainder of McCleery's gang followed him into the darkness.

'OK, we got two of 'em. Good shootin', Mr Farney!' Todd exclaimed.

'Wouldn't have been possible without the support of the team here,' Dwight Farney said, pointing to Trixie-Lou and Nat. 'Using a Gatling successfully is a team effort. No room for individual lone ranger stuff.'

'So what's the next move, then, boss?' Abe enquired, looking at Todd. 'What do you think McCleery will do next?'

'I think he'll have another go at attacking the new town. So I think most of you should stay here an' stick to our defence plan. There's still four of 'em, an' consequently I think McCleery might regroup and have another go. If he loses another man or two, I'll reckon he'll get the hell out of here, at least until he can put a bigger gang together an' that'll take time. Zac an' me will go into the old town an' see if we can't speed up McCleery's departure.'

23

Although the preacher knew how to fire a gun and in fact owned a Sharps buffalo rifle — part of the very small inheritance left to him by his father — he had never fired one at a human being or an animal come to that. After all, it was against his religion. Still, he had the rifle with him now. He regarded its presence as a potential deterrent against being attacked and that boosted his confidence for the small mission he had decided to undertake as a contribution to the town's war effort.

He had caught sight of the McCleery gang scurrying away into the dark shadows of the network of alleyways that made up the red light district. Normally, this place would have been ablaze with light coming from inside people's homes and their businesses. But not tonight. There was only the odd light here or there and the preacher felt more people had stayed behind than this particular measure indicated. Although a risky endeavour, he figured that if he knocked on doors and persuaded those who might be cowering in the darkness to turn on their lights, it would be easier for McFarlane and the sheriff to find McCleery. It would also help salve his conscience and make amends; although his natural role was to talk, advise and mediate — valuable, but passive activities, he felt that when it came to decisive action, he had let himself and the townsfolk down and been found wanting.

★   ★   ★

'There's various lights goin' on,' Zac pointed out as he and Todd entered the maze of alleyways and back streets that made up the old quarter of Morton's Cross.

'Strange,' Todd commented. 'Seems a

bit random.' They walked on in silence for a few minutes, keeping to the shadows as much as possible.

'Dunno if it's a good thing or not,' Zac continued. 'Don't know if we are better off with the light or in darkness. If you were McCleery what would you do right now? Would you make a break for it, regroup somewhere away from here and come back later on?'

'Dunno where they've left their horses but if they intend gettin' the hell out of here, in this damned silence we'd hear the noise of the hooves as they galloped away. That would turn this battle into a race. I don't think that's McCleery's style. I reckon he'll hole up here — there are plenty of places to hide an' wait for us. If you were desperate, Zac, where would you hide?' McFarlane asked. 'I dunno this part of town.'

'Up the top, at the back there,' Zac replied, pointing ahead. 'You notice the streets are slowly climbing towards the cliff face at the back of this part of town. Well, there's a ledge at the bottom of the cliff face. The water storage tanks for this part of town are mounted on stilts on that ledge. It's the highest point of the old quarter. It's Farney and Royston's water. It flows down the escarpment and into the storage tanks at the station. Those tanks serve the railroad and the new part of town. A steam pump pumps water from there to the storage tanks up here. The old quarter then gets its water by gravity feed. That's why the tanks are situated at the highest point. But the highest point also offers a good view. Not only that but it's a protected view. A man can conceal himself quite easily up there.'

'That all makes good sense,' Todd said. 'But it looks like someone is lighting our path up there. If you look at the patterns of these seemingly random lights going on, it's like a zigzag up the ascent to those tanks. Could be a trap. We should work our way up along one of the sides. Less likely to be seen then.'

'Good thinkin', Todd. I know the best route. I'll show yer,' Zac said. McFarlane followed Riley up the ascent, both men carrying a rifle in one hand and a six-shooter in the other.

★ ★ ★

'What are these, boss?' asked one of the four remaining members of the McCleery gang, tapping the large metal cylinder above his head.

'Water tanks,' McCleery whispered. 'Part of the town's water supply.'

'Should we destroy 'em?' another of the outlaws said.

'No,' McCleery replied. 'If these are damaged the water still gets to town. They'll jest rig up some sort of standpipe until the tanks are repaired. It's a far easier proposition than dealing with a break in the supply pipe out on the escarpment. Besides, there's hardly anyone here. Whoever's left won't worry about no water to drink as long as they've got whiskey. The whiskey's probably healthier if the water's been putrefying in these tanks for a while. Keep an eye on the lit areas, men, but watch the shadows. If I understand the mind o' that McFarlane, he'd have already worked out we will be up here an' on his way. But he won't come out of the lit areas.'

'So who's lightin' up them houses?' one of the outlaws said.

'It's that preacher thinkin' he's bein' helpful to McFarlane whereas in fact he is bein' more helpful to us.' McCleery grinned at the thought. 'I know exactly whereabouts he is. I don't wanna take him out right now 'cos it will give our exact position away.'

'What was that?' one of the outlaws demanded to know.

'What was what?'

'That noise.' They listened closely. It was coming from the shadows.

★ ★ ★

The preacher moved behind the cover of a rock. From his position to the side of the water tanks he could see the McCleery gang quite easily. They had to crouch down together to keep in the shadow of the tanks now that some lights had been switched on in the houses of the nearest street. The preacher could also make out the silhouettes of Todd McFarlane and Zac Riley. But he could see they were in trouble, unaware of exactly how close they were to the McCleery gang. The four outlaws, however, had their guns trained on the spot in the bushes from which Todd and Zac would emerge.

The preacher raised the Sharps buffalo rifle to his shoulder. To the unknowing, it looked as if the man with the dog collar was about to pull the trigger on a group of fellow human beings at a range of twenty yards. But the preacher's god had not forsaken him. The bullet from the Sharps tore through one of the wooden supporting legs and pierced the tank's thin skin. As the tank toppled over, water started gushing from the bullet hole, the pressurized stream turning into a torrent, as the metal casing split apart on contact with the ground.

* * *

'Well, I'll be damned,' said Zac Riley, dropping to the ground. 'It's the preacher. He has really turned up trumps this time!'

'He sure has!' said Todd as he opened fire on the McCleery gang with his six-shooter. He found his target with the third bullet. It hit one of the sodden outlaws in the stomach. He staggered around for a few seconds, totally disoriented, before falling into a pool of water, turning it a pale red colour. Zac Riley hit the second outlaw in the chest, who fell off the ledge, crashing to his death on the jagged stone street, twelve feet below. The third outlaw lay on the ground unconscious, at the edge of the pool, its blood-coloured water lapping at his body.

And that left McCleery. Although hit by the falling support structure, he had missed the torrent of water and had managed to sustain fire with his two six-shooters. But he now had no one to give him covering fire while he reloaded. And he didn't want to give himself up and return to prison again. The firing had stopped. For McCleery it was the last chance saloon. He pulled a stick of dynamite from his dry coat pocket and lit the fuse. Hearing the fizzing noise, Todd McFarlane realized that he had seconds before it was thrown. Standing up, he saw McCleery's left arm pull back ready to throw the explosive. As he rose to his feet, McFarlane pulled the trigger and then fell back down to the ground. The bullet pierced through McCleery's left wrist. He dropped the lit stick of dynamite and froze in pain. The preacher crossed his chest and hid down behind his rock. There was a massive explosion.

'Live by the sword, die by the sword,' Zac Riley said as the smoke cleared.

'I guess so,' said Todd McFarlane.

Epilogue

The next day, the townsfolk of Morton's Cross returned to their homes. Both the new town and the old quarter took on something of a carnival atmosphere. Although Trixie-Lou Sanders would have been more than happy to stay and join in the revelry, it didn't suit the style of the new man in her life, Todd McFarlane. Todd was a professional. Having conducted the elimination of the McCleery gang, he had completed his work in Morton's Cross and it was time to move on.

'I can't thank you enough, Mr McFarlane,' Dwight Farney said. 'You pulled us all back together when we were starting to lose it between ourselves.'

'Thank you, Mr Mayor,' Todd replied. 'But I didn't do that. You did that. McCleery put you all, in your own way, under extreme psychological pressure. That's what really bad men do. It's siege mentality. They force you to face your demons. Many people go under but the leaders of Morton's Cross refused to do that. With grit and stoicism, you all took on your shadow side and stepped up. It was that spirit — your spirit — that meant I had a team I could lead and co-ordinate.'

'You're very kind, Mr McFarlane, Miss Sanders,' Dwight Farney said, doffing his hat to the lady. 'Where are you off to?'

'San Francisco,' Trixie-Lou said. 'Time to take on the big city! Myself as an actress and Todd here to widen his career in terms of law enforcement. The frontier is fast disappearing. In a few years it will no longer exist, so it is time to prepare and adapt, ready for when that day comes.'

'They are profound words, Miss Sanders, profound indeed,' Dwight Farney commented thoughtfully. 'If I may be so bold and pray forgive me for asking, but did you have to face any inner demons during this siege of our town?'

'Sure did, Mr Mayor,' Trixie-Lou exclaimed readily. 'As an actress, I am a lady of many roles and many personalities but I have discovered the one underneath them all that is really me. And I am glad to say that I really like her!'

'Bravo!' Dwight Farney said, with a sincere smile on his face. 'And you, sir?'

'I guess I needed to do something similar,' Todd said. 'Been too long valuin' my work more than meself. I needed to find a teacher help me do that. And thanks to Morton's Cross, I have.' He gesticulated towards Trixie-Lou.

'Well done, both of you, and good luck.'

'Good luck to you, too, and all the people of Morton's Cross,' Todd said as he and Trixie-Lou wheeled their horses round and rode out of town.

We do hope that you have enjoyed reading this large print book.

Did you know that all of our titles are available for purchase?

We publish a wide range of high quality large print books including:
Romances, Mysteries, Classics
General Fiction
Non Fiction and Westerns

Special interest titles available in large print are:
The Little Oxford Dictionary
Music Book, Song Book
Hymn Book, Service Book

Also available from us courtesy of Oxford University Press:
Young Readers' Dictionary
(large print edition)
Young Readers' Thesaurus
(large print edition)

For further information or a free brochure, please contact us at:
Ulverscroft Large Print Books Ltd.,
The Green, Bradgate Road, Anstey,
Leicester, LE7 7FU, England.
Tel: (00 44) 0116 236 4325
Fax: (00 44) 0116 234 0205

Other titles in the
Linford Western Library:

CHISHOLM TRAIL
SHOWDOWN

Jack Tregarth

For the young men in the Texas town of Indian Falls, riding the Chisholm Trail as cowboys is a rite of passage. Dan Lewis is heartbroken when it looks as though he is to be cheated of his chance. Determinedly, he manages to secure a place on the trail, but his joy quickly fades as he is accused of cattle rustling and nearly lynched. As he fights to clear his name, he finds himself up against a gang of the most ruthless men in the state . . .

LAND OF THE SAINTS

Jay Clanton

It is the summer of 1858, and the Turner family are making their way along the Oregon Trail to California. The wagon train with which they are travelling is attacked by a band of Paiute, but this is no mere skirmish in the Indian Wars. The territory of Utah, or Deseret as those who live there call it, is in open rebellion against the government in Washington. Turner and his wife and daughter are caught in the crossfire of what is turning out to be a regular shooting war.